NEW DIRECTIONS 45

In memoriam
KENNETH REXROTH
1905–1982

N D

New Directions in Prose and Poetry 45

Edited by J. Laughlin

with Peter Glassgold and Frederick R. Martin

 A New Directions Book

ACKNOWLEDGMENTS
Grateful acknowledgment is made to the editors and publishers of books and magazines in which some of the material in this volume first appeared: for Bian Zhilin, *Chinese Literature* (Beijing); for Fumiko Enchi, *Rabbits, Crabs, Etc.*, University of Hawaii Press (Copyright © 1982 by Phyllis Birnbaum); for Lawrence Ferlinghetti, *Harper's Magazine* (Copyright © 1981 by the Harper's Magazine Foundation); for James B. Hall, *The Georgia Review* (Copyright © 1982 by the University of Georgia); for Harold Jaffe, *Mourning Crazy Horse*, Fiction Collective, Inc. (Copyright © 1982 by Harold Jaffe); for Reiner Kunze, *zimmerlautstärke/with the volume down low*, Swamp Press (Oneonta, N.Y.) (Copyright © S. Fischer Verlag GmbH, Frankfort am Main, 1972), *Buckle* (Copyright © 1980 by Buckle), *Footprint* (Copyright © 1980 by Footprint Magazine).

Max Aub's "El Manuscrito del Cuervo ("The Manuscript of a Crow"), included in *Cuentos Ciertos*, © Max Aub, 1955

James Laughlin's "The River," Copyright 1938 by New Directions

Manufactured in the United States of America
First published clothbound (ISBN: 0–8112–0844–3) and as New Directions Paperbook 541 (ISBN: 0–8112–0845–1) in 1982
Published simultaneously in Canada by George J. McLeod, Ltd., Toronto

New Directions Books are published for James Laughlin
by New Directions Publishing Corporation,
80 Eighth Avenue, New York 10011

CONTENTS

TALL TALE OF THE TALL COWBOY

LAWRENCE FERLINGHETTI

How the Great Cowboy rode to the Rio Grande
and gave the President of Mexico
a hunting rifle a bad omen
How the great Cowboy took over from the Great Charmer
who faded away into Georgia to be born again
How they lined up at the Rio Grande to take their stand
How they lined up at the great trough across the land
How they reconquered the West and resettled Washington
How the Metternich of Foggy Bottom
still moved behind the scenes
How they anointed generals to run countries
How they redrew the maps of the known world
How they forgot the barrios North and South
How they lassoed the red lions of Latin America
How the Great Cowboy ruled over all with a schoolboy grin
How his lady had a handgun with a pearl handle
How his tall shadow reached over the Rio Grande
How they gave human rights back to the right rulers
How they gave the land back to the old guarders
How the high rollers got back in the saddles again
How the Great Cowboy shook his head with a sheepish grin
for the benefit of a nation of sheep
How they reversed the irreversible revolutions

How they corraled the tough hombres North and South
How they buffaloed both sides
How they gave them bullets to bite
How they swallowed hard
when the Great Cowboy laughed on TV
How the Great Cowboy waved his hand
and disappeared over the horizon
How he walked softly and carried a big nuke
How he brandished it like a hunting rifle
How the President of Mexico gave him a great stallion
How he tried to mount it as the cameras rolled
How he slung his hunting rifle behind him and swung up
How the people hid in their houses
How the hot sun beat down on the mined land of the world
How the swinging-door saloons stood empty and silent
How the natives were restless and beat their drums
in the concrete jungles of the world
How the Indians said How Come instead of How
How the Indians hid in the hills
How the Great Smiler smiled no more on TV
How he came on his great white stallion
propped up from behind with a big stick
How he stood tall in the saddle
and looked straight into the cameras
How the old hands hid in the old corrals
How the deputies deputized themselves
and took to the roofs
How the people trembled in their houses
How they thought it was the final shoot-out
How a great hush fell upon the plazas of the world
How the Great Cowboy put on one black glove
How his eyes narrowed and his hand reached behind him
How suddenly there was nowhere to hide
How suddenly there was no turning back
How suddenly it was High Noon

THE MANUSCRIPT OF A CROW: JACOB'S STORY

MAX AUB

Translated from the Spanish and introduced by Will Kirkland

INTRODUCTION

The reputation of Max Aub, one of Spain's great novelists and story-tellers, a literary talent of the first order, is another tragedy among the many to come out of the Spanish Civil War of 1936–39. Exiled in Mexico where he wrote his master work, *The Magic Labyrinth*—the *War and Peace* of Spain, as it has been called—he was censored in his homeland until after Franco's death in 1975. It was only then that his work appeared and could be read and acknowledged by the people he wrote for. Because of the long interval, and Aub's own death in 1972, he may never receive the acclaim that is due him. We know, however, when we enter his fictional-historical worlds that we are in the company of a great writer and a great man.

Born in 1902 in Paris of a German father and a French mother, he moved with them to Valencia, Spain, when he was eleven years old. There he adopted Spanish as his language and revealed himself as a writer and dramatist. The advent of the Civil War brought him first to edit a Republican newspaper, then to become the cultural attaché for the Republic in Paris, and later to work with André Malraux on a film about the war for distribution in the United

States to raise funds for the beleagured Republicans. With the fall of the Republic, he was captured and jailed by Franco's forces.

Kept in concentration camps in Paris, Vernet, and Djelfa (Algeria), he eventually escaped to Mexico. It is in the Vernet camp that the marvelous *Jacob's Story* unfolds. Adopting a favorite ruse, Aub claims to have come across a real manuscript of which he is only the humble carrier. In this case, the manuscript is of a translation into Spanish of the anthropological notes of an erudite crow, written originally in the corvine language. The crow, taking his point of view in the camp as equivalent to one of all men in general, offers us a series of "field notes" that are delightful, wry, sad, and hopeless at the same time. We are moved betwixt and between, laughing first at the crow's anthropological naïveté that takes his skewed sample as representative of all human beings (reminding us in the process of similarly biased samples and outrageous claims made by human ethnographers) and then feeling stunned when we realize that in fact all men are very much like those men, that the naïveté has yielded quite salient results.

We find here many of Aub's recurring themes: a commitment to the good, yet in the face of the (momentarily) inevitable the wisdom to acquiesce, an acquiesence lightened with irony, a well-placed phrase, or a sturdy shrug of the shoulders. Always part of the swirling Spanish left, Aub could step back and see underneath the interminable debates, claims, and promises the eternal human currents of venality, self-interest, and misguided good intentions; he saw this and yet found no reason for giving way to despair or cynicism.

Jacob's Story, along with *The Bootblack of Our Eternal Father*, another story about the postwar camps for Republicans, was written in 1941 and first appeared in print in 1950. In 1955, it appeared in its final form in a collection titled *Cuentos Ciertos*. The English translation here has been somewhat edited for length and topical references that might make it less lively for English-speaking readers.

THE MANUSCRIPT OF A CROW

JACOB'S STORY

Editing, prologue, and notes by
J. R. Brouhaha
A chronicler of his country and a visitor to a few more

Dedicated to those who knew the selfsame Jacob
in the Vernet camp,
who were not a few in numbers

*Translated now for the first time from the
corvine language by Aben Maximo
Albarrón*

PROLOGUE

> In fact works of divine act have I don't
> know what sort of beauty, hidden and
> secret as it were, so that however often
> looked at, they always bring new plea-
> sure.
>
> J. José de Acosta, S.J.
> (*The Natural and Moral History of the
> Indies*)

When I left the concentration camp at Vernet, for the first time, and arrived in Toulouse in the last months of 1940, I found a note-book in my suitcase which I had not put there.

Jacob had disappeared some days earlier and nothing was known of him, nor, as I found out later, was news of him ever again heard. Jacob was a well-trained crow whose greatest skill was in perching on the lids of vats full of waste, our own and others, which we car-ried to the river to empty and clean with the constancy and regu-larity worthy of a far better cause. He used to stroll about between the barracks, showing off a bit and even flew from A to B and C, the camps we were divided into by chance, although in the begin-ning the first corresponded to those they called "politicos," the last to common criminals, and the other to riffraff of the most varied sort: Jews, Spanish Republicans, a Polish count, undocumented Hun-garians, anti-Fascist Italians, soldiers from the International Brigades, vagabonds, professors, etc.

I don't know who put that notebook in my baggage. I did not personally have any relations with Jacob. These pages have gone all over the world, *idem* myself, according to the chances of fortune. If I am now giving them to the printer it is only as a bibliographic curiosity and memory of a time past, that, as they say, will never return, as it is now well known by everyone that wars and concen-tration camps are over with.

It is evident that it was Jacob's idea to write a treatment of how men live, for the benefit of his own species. As it seems, either he didn't have time to finish it, or it is no more than the first draft of the book published in the corvine language. The table of contents, which is at the beginning of the notebook, promises more than is in the text, which is not, of course, a purely corvine weakness; let he who has not laid out a table of contents that never saw the morning raise his hand.

DESCRIPTION OF THE MANUSCRIPT: 34 pages of a notebook which has 48; 18 by 24 centimeters, written in strange letters (see the facsimile) which are not, however, difficult to decipher. The cover is red, and on the back is a multiplication table. The front reads, *L'Incomparable*, and underneath, *48 pages.*

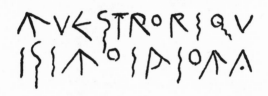

↑	Transcribed M
∧	Transcribed N, the foot influence (it is clear)
ʃ	Transcribed S (the wormy preoccupation is evident)
↚	Transcribed E
∧	Transcribed A

On the procedures for substitutions see the Mss. in the cathedral of Seville.

Copulative Signs: The angle imprinted as E.

Abbreviations: They have been written out insofar as it was possible for me.

I would like to give my most express thanks to His Excellency Monsieur Roy, Minister of the Interior, a socialist as I am, who, in 1940 was good enough to help me to take on the manuscript and gave me the time and leisure necessary, and even a little unnecessary, to decipher it.

J.R.B.

Marseilles the 25th of June, 1946

CONTENTS

[1] A North American, who doubts nothing, had the nerve, in inscribing
his work, to assert that *All God's Children Have Wings.* What gods, what
children, what wings?

PRELIMINARY CONSIDERATIONS OF MYSELF

Everything leads one to presume that I belong to the most illustrious corvine family. If my extraordinary destiny didn't give credit to it, my physical appearance would tell all: good stature, sparkling eyes, lustrous coat, aquiline beak, aggressive foot, noble carriage, strident caw. My destiny has brought me to discover and look over regions which, even if seen before, were never understood by my fellow creatures. This brings me to take the quill by the beak, for the enlightenment of the rest.

My birth is wrapped in the darkest of mysteries, which is proof of my illustrious heritage. I made myself. If such modesty be permitted to me, I owe nothing to anyone. My first memories coincide with my relations with the bipeds, though in the dimness of my mind remains engraved, as though at the beginning of my life and deeds, the stamp of an extremely long fall from the very heights of the heavens.

If I judge it to be necessary to inform my compatriots of the strange customs and usages which I here present it is, in the first place, because it gives me the crowing pleasure; in the second, for the glory that I will surely carry away from this enterprise; and, thirdly, for the benefit of such crows as there may be in the world.

If, on the other hand, these lines reach human eyes, I have to ask forgiveness. With your pardon: the fact is I don't know where I was born. I consider this aspect of things very important because men have determined that the place where they first see light is of transcendental import for their futures. That is to say, if instead of being born in nest A you are born in nest B the conditions of life will change entirely and completely. If you are born in Peking you are declared Chinese, for good or bad. In the very same way, if you are Buenos Airean you are held to be Argentinian, be you white or black or yellow or copper. Add passports for even more clarity. Can you imagine a crow being French or Spanish because of having been born on one side of the Pyrenees or the other?

I am, then, truly hesitant to present myself to men without knowing where I am from, though I came out of an egg, as is natural, and the son of unknown parents. Seen from the human angle a person who doesn't know where he was born or who his parents are is a dangerous being. It is a good thing that I'm a crow because, if not, I would have already been assigned a label: if a man is English his parents can't have been other than honest people, they look at him with respect; all Spaniards are sons of bullfighters; the Italians, sons of singers; the Germans, sons of professors; Corsicans, sons of Mobile Guards; if Chinese, sons of rice, the only ones who spring up by spontaneous generation. That is to say, their paternity and natal earth are somehow unified, the result no doubt of some very ancient rites. Each area of land is symbolized by colorful flags which vary according to the times and the dominant factions.

OF THEIR GODS

Men do what they don't want to do. In order to arrive at this end, so absurd by our lights, they have invented those who will give them orders. But these latter, in turn, don't do what they want either, but what they are ordered. Those who give the most orders don't do exactly what they want either because they are always dependent on an obscure force, perhaps invented by them, called Bureaucracy. The Lie and the Bureaucracy are the gods of those on the outside, that is to say, of the inferior caste which gives orders to their superiors, the internees.

OF WORK

A most curious animal, which having four usable extremities only uses two to get about, so demonstrating the embryonic state of his cerebrum. I have heard through reliable sources that to the south, in places still prohibited to our species,[2] there lives another class of

[2] I am referring, of course, to the great fire in the belly of the Great Red Crow, down below the great sheet of the Great Yellow Crow, which men call the Sahara. It seems that it is only there that there exists a certain possibility of the regeneration of the human species. They say that in these

man, which is a little more rational; they are called monkeys and are of a variety of species; although they waste fifty percent of their motive power they are justified by the element in which they live: forests, where what they call hands are good for grasping vines, branches, trunks, etc. . . .

The degeneration of man is noticed principally in these parts of their structure: they are good for nothing, unless it is to corrupt them: a) either selling themselves for *money*, which they take with an open hand, or b) working; this latter being a plague exclusive to man and which, thanks to the Great Crow, does not spread beyond those here in the foreground, who undergo a slow decline that makes them voluntarily submit themselves to doing all sorts of absolutely useless exercises from when they begin to have use of their reason and are strong enough until they die, so powerful is the vice.* They are so lost, so without their heads that they turn in circles, climb around, pound, break into pieces, undo, mistreat whatever comes into their hands, solely in order to tire themselves out. Instead of marveling at what the Great Crow has given us, they are dedicated—under his eyes—to trampling on it; in place of not having eyes for such beauty, they sometimes—oh sign of negligence!—try to reproduce it (with results that are always lamentable, as they could not otherwise be). Instead of sitting down and resting, and praising the one who gave it all to us, they try, in their congenital imbecility, to transform—impoverishing it in the attempt—such magnificence. Their pleasures are pitched into pits in proportion to their efforts. They call this *working*. Their aberration has reached such a degree that, not content with their own personal

---

lower latitudes, in the heat of the Great Red Crow, a new type of man is being shaped which, seeing our superiority, is trying to make a better copy of our way of being. Though at the moment it has only occurred to them—and this is comprehensible given the laggard mentality that impedes them—to imitate us in the most simple way: in color; there, at this moment, exist black men. I have seen them. I, of course, am not prejudiced, but without a doubt, and I postpone the proofs: the whiter the men—they call it blond—the more barbarous and savage. This is a problem regarding the epidermal pigmentation of humans which I cannot at the moment pause to examine.

* A reference to gymnastics? (Translator's note)

flight from leisure, there are those who make the others work. They call this *business*. Of course the *businessmen* are the most despicable human caste. Such a sickness has brought this unhappy race to believe that they have to earn something in order to eat. I don't have space here to examine words like *workday, office, occupation,* which are absolutely untranslatable into our idiom. Nevertheless I don't want to forget to take note of their expression: *To earn a living,* because it shows the extent to which their comprehension of things has been corrupted. And that other one—which is completely esoteric—*You shall earn your bread by the sweat of your brow.* As if bread had to be earned or had anything to do with sweat or brows. It is a magic formula which, to my trustworthy knowledge and understanding, is at the base of the almost inconceivable backwardness of this curious species.

They steal hours from sleep to break up the earth, amusing themselves by leveling it, opening holes, in drilling into mountains, day and night they sweat, doing useless work, carving wood, casting metals, sweeping streets, running after a ball. Nothing of all this is functional. And so they go, fuming about their world, as if it weren't they themselves that had shaped their slavery. *Convicts, peasants, laborers, secretaries, foremen, sellers, farmhands, overseers, managers, metalworkers, artisans, apprentices,* as these and a thousand other ways they are called, according to their work: all of them, mercenaries.

Nor is all this the worst. They have convinced some other species with no more brains to set themselves to imitating them, or even exceed them: mules, dogs, oxen, horses. It is not to no purpose it is said: to work like a mule.

OF THE EXCELLENCES OF THE CAMPS

Confinement improves the human condition. In order to make men quite excellent they are usually locked up for a certain period of time.

When the men in command don't spend a little while in an advanced school of this kind, an epoch of decadence emerges, nearing the end of the cycle; the big bosses are dethroned by people who have come from the jails and the concentration camps.

ON HIERARCHIES

Once again I find myself facing the impossible task of trying to explain one of the fundamentals of human society. How could a crow begin to comprehend that another crow is worth more than he is, or less, when both are crows? All crows are black, and that is that. Men wear signs of their status on their exteriors, so there can be no room for doubt. They are valued according to, and for, their stripes. (A stripe is a ribbon, a strip of cloth, put on the sleeves of their uniforms; it is important to realize that silver is as noteworthy an invention as gold. They also hang medals from their chests, feudalizing the wills of those who do not possess them.)* The tone of voice varies according to these stripes, of which the internees have none at all. Those who have more stripes order around those who have less; and they, those who have none. So from top to bottom they unload their anger: the general on the colonel; the colonel on the major; the major on the captain; the captain on the lieutenant; the lieutenant on the second lieutenant; the second lieutenant on the sergeant; the sergeant on the corporal; the corporal on the private. But then the German private orders around the French general, as was said earlier. And everyone orders around the internees, to make sure they learn, just in case they don't already understand; but it's always good to pound it into them. And they are pounded on.

* This parenthetical remark seems to be an insertion in the hand of a magpie. (Translator's note)

OF MONEY

No one can understand men without penetrating the great mystery of money and the theory of value. It must be recognized, very frankly, as a very very notable invention; it would be worth the trouble for it alone to embark on a study of this species which has otherwise come to be so little.

The fact is that, mislead by his manifest inadequacy thousands of years ago, man suddenly left off respecting himself for what he was (what he was in himself, truly) in order to think about what he was *worth:* his value. This gyration, this twisting about, brought him by the hand to the invention of a symbol in order to approximately fix that value. So it quickly came to be that everyone was catalogued according to the various estimates of their leaders: you are worth this much; you are worth that much; you aren't worth anything; you are worth a lot.

The unit was called money. Due to the diversity of languages this standard took on different names, all of them beautiful: the onza, ducat, doubloon, florin, real, maravedi, escudo, peso, sol, dollar, aguila,[3] etc. As can be seen, everything in the world is represented by these names: birds, flowers, countries, stars. It could be no other way: with this simple conversion a price was placed on everything. The shiniest metals were consecrated to standing for that ideal; their value was minted according to weight. Then by transmutation the value of that which was represented was lost and was transformed into intrinsic value; men were no longer valued for what they were, but for what they accumulated.

This inevitable progression is now carrying humanity toward a better end: the day in which all metals will be in the hands of one person or nation and the onerous discussions will be over—those that have contributed so much to the degeneration of the species— by the fact that men, having invented money,[4] have spent their lives

[3] Names of various coins, each embossed with figures such as horse and rider, lion, lily, eagle (W.K.).

[4] I don't want to go into the mystery of money, capital, interest, the stock market, etc., right here, given that each of these concepts deserves a separate study. I hope these brief lines will waken the interest of a few studious crows and we might look forward to some good monographs about them soon.

arguing over it and killing each other to possess it. When they don't dare commit crimes directly, they resort to what is humorously called "paid labor." So it was that slavery was invented. Recently a certain tribe has risen up against this—they speak Esperanto—called Anarchists, but without much success. And now others have begun a new crusade against money.[5] This very concentration camp from which I am writing proves it.[6]

They have come together here to try to work without being paid. As to the results of this procedure, it is still too early to determine the full consequences. Nevertheless, despite the excellence of the proposals I can see that the men are getting skinnier and are as wrinkled as parchment, although this being drawn down inside themselves may be simply the exteriorization of a greater spirituality. But neither do they seem very satisfied, or happy—although laughter may be a very inferior manifestation of that. I have heard it said that in Germany camps of this same kind exist, and with the same purpose, at the entrances of which can be read: "Work for Happiness." That is to say that men are trying to exchange money for smiles. I can't answer for the truth of it of course; it will have to be verified. (To pass on to Professor A ZI–40 in the Black Forest.)

The bank note or paper money (to which I refer in another place) was invented later. I haven't been able to find out why that printed in England is worth more than others, but it is a fact. A man who is well loaded with dollars (a specie I haven't been able to see) is worth what he weighs, and even more.[7]

Another human subspecies exists about which I have no exact reports: counterfeiters. I have seen some of the counterfeit money made by this group. In my judgment it is no different than all the rest. The bankers treat them like criminals and hate them, just as the Communists hate the Trotskyists, or Prieto's socialists those of Negrin, or vice versa—complications I will try to explain further on. *

[5] Their great book is called *Capital*, which, contrary to what the title might make you suppose, is directed totally against what it proclaims. Men are impossible to understand.

[6] Concentration; that is to say, the most examinable, the core, the substance.

[7] In order to know what a man is worth he is weighed and measured as soon as he is taken in by the police, which is a subsidiary organization of the banks.

* Something he didn't do, or perhaps the papers were lost. (Translator's note)

OF EYEGLASSES

The only custom men have that would seem to me to be useful for the corvine civilization is in their employment of eyeglasses. Being a typical feature of the most peaceful and intelligent, they would be a likely thing to adopt as they tell us from a distance those who we should most respect. I have not yet given up hope of meeting a crow optician some day—that is the name given among men to those who bestow this honor. The said objects consist of two transparent medals, spectacles, that are placed on the beak and in front of the eyes so everyone can see them perfectly well. They give an air of distinction and, furthermore, the wearer cannot forget his select position. They aren't to see in, but to be seen in.

OF ARMS

From everything I know, man has come to be, and every day is still coming to be, less. He is the only being to have invented what they call arms. That is to say, instruments with which to kill like cowards, without exposing themselves. They respect us, as they can't help but doing, because of our ancestral superiority, but only let them speak of rabbits, hares, quail, or of men themselves—because their greatest concern is to kill each other. They say that in remote ages, as would be natural and the only justification, they did it in order to eat the victim. Today, not so. They are content with burying them. According to vague rumors I have heard I understand that some dark-colored tribes still continue that ancient and rational custom. The superiority of the physical appearance of these latter has to be recognized from the one way in which they are similar to us (in color), though in that alone; a crow, of course, never eats nor will ever eat another crow.

OF POLITICS

Definition: the art of direction.

Means: make hypocrisy a virtue. (Those who can't do this are called sectarians, biased, fanatics; or suckers, simpletons, and idiots.)

Example:

"Who? So and so? He's a jackass."

Enter So and So:

"My dear So and so! Long time no see! Where've you been keeping yourself?"

OF QUANTITY

Men need to count and recount themselves to know how many of them there are. Four times a day they group together, get into lines and answer: *Present,* on hearing their name. It would be better for them to know how they are.

OF WARS

Wars are always lost, sometimes by a little, other times by a lot; some in weeks, others in years. War is the natural state of human relations. They are lost along with life, sometimes without noticing, others in full lucidity; it depends more on the circumstances than on the understandings. There are those who die like gentlemen and gentlemen who die without the least shame, howling like dogs. In order to help them die, well or badly, they invent recompenses, which like everything of its kind is imaginary.

Failure to learn from experience is another of the characteristics of man: So many years for nothing! Wars come from those in command—say some—and as those who are made to command not to fight are the generals, they foment them against the general populace, which fights and doesn't command. The generals, conquered or conquerors—which, is not important—quarrel over the spoils. There was a time, spoken of by their forebears, when there were wars disputing over only one cadaver. This, which makes sense to us, has passed into legend for men.[8]

OF FASCISM

The human world is now separated in two parts: those who fight for and those who fight against Fascism. From the empirical point of view everything is clear, but my thirst for knowledge, my curiosity has pushed me—for the greater glory of science—to verify what it is that this apple of discord consists of. I give you here the partial results of my investigation:

The Fascists are racists and don't permit Jews to wash or eat with Aryans.

The anti-Fascists are not racists and don't permit Negroes to wash or eat with whites.[9]

The Fascists put yellow stars on the sleeves of the Jews.

The anti-Fascists don't do that, a black face is enough for them.

The Fascists put anti-Fascists in concentration camps.

The anti-Fascists put anti-Fascists in concentration camps.

The Fascists don't allow strikes.

The anti-Fascists put an end to strikes with bullets.

[8] I owe this imprecise information to a Jehovah's Witness, though I couldn't confirm it, and many deny it.

[9] Written in 1941 and certainly before the 22nd of June (ed.). (After much searching I am still perplexed by this date. I conclude that it is: 1) meant to perplex the reader; 2) the date of the German invasion of Russia, and the editor, making assumptions on behalf of the disappeared author, is implying he wouldn't have made such a remark had he known the changed conditions; or, 3) a reference to F.D.R.'s Executive Order 8802, of June 25, 1941, reaffirming the U.S. War Department policy of no discrimination because of race, color, etc. W.K.)

The Fascists control industry directly.

The anti-Fascists control industry indirectly.

The Fascists can live in anti-Fascist countries.

The anti-Fascists cannot live in Fascist countries or in some anti-Fascist countries either.

OF THE COMMUNISTS

They are very much to be admired according to the photographs I have seen; they display more stars, more medals, more decorations than anyone. They absolutely shine.

OF LOGIC

The internees were brought here by one administration. This administration has disappeared, but the men are still here. Another administration succeeded the first one, and it brought in more internees. As the first cannot make any demands on the administration that brought them here, since it no longer exists, they have no one to direct their solicitations for liberty to, and so they will stay here until they die.

OF NATIONALITY

Sometimes the internees change nationality without chewing or swallowing. They go to sleep Poles and wake up Russian. They lie down Rumanians and get up Soviets. Internees at night, in the morning free. They didn't have a passport, and now they have one.

Mysteries of borders and pacts. Nicolai and Alexei Tisanoff, two brothers, born in two Polish villages, ten kilometers between them, woke up this morning, one of them free, the other a prisoner, due to a new frontier. Witchspells of the imagination.

OF ALPARGATAS

Men, from walking so much, and due to the lack of wings, cannot go with their feet unshod. They cover them with the carrion of dead animals, calling them shoes. It should be acknowledged that it saves them a little from the water and the mud. The Red Cross sent five hundred pairs of alpargatas to the camp to be distributed among the internees; they are canvas shoes and better than nothing. They have them in the store rooms, under guard, waiting for who knows what. An old man, Eloy Pinto, sixty-five years old, a butcher and lame, asked for a pair of good boots from a young guard. They made him sweep and wash the cuartel, telling him to come back the next day, that they would give him the alpargatas. The scene was repeated for eight days. The old man, tired by now, asked the adjutant for them:

"Hah! So you want alpargatas, do you? And you don't want to work. But eating, you eat of course, don't you? You're not absent from the food line, are you?"

The old man fell quiet, looked at his feet wrapped up in rags, and slowly raised his eyes. The adjutant spat in his face and continued:

"I suppose your conscience is clean, huh? Isn't that what you think? Well put it on your feet."

OF RAIN

The internees suffer the rain well. They form up to take muster in the pouring-down rain. The guards, with raincoats, arrive late. The prisoners don't move; the water runs down their faces; it soaks them; they don't protest. When it rains the men don't wash.

OF THE CONDITIONS FOR LEAVING

As is natural, with such good treatment, the men don't want to leave the concentration camps. Those in uniforms do whatever is necessary to make them happy.

The first condition that is necessary to leave is to have been detained in a *free zone* [10] and, by what is said here, ninety-five percent of those gathered here were in *occupied zones*.

Second: to have the consent of the prefect of the area where they are going to live.

Third: to demonstrate that they have a means of livelihood.

Fourth: to have had good conduct.

If by chance one of the prescribed conditions is present, the rest never get assembled. No one leaves, unless feet first.

[10] I don't know what it is.

FIFTEEN POEMS

CID CORMAN

1

We love that Hamlet
whose hesitancy
betrays our own trust—

who wont easily
kill what he must hate
and wouldnt at all

but for the mistake
of his own life called
beyond further bluff.

We know Arjuna's
difficulty. Death
begins to wean us

from ourselves. What we
have to do 's bound to
drive us up the wall

and gradually
over it as well
into Krishna's hands.

In the meanwhile we—
in our own guises—have
ghosts to listen to.

2

Myself: pocked pimpled
skin—doubling chin—
mouth straight and thin—eyes

knit by wrinkle—
forehead almost all
gone to skull. But

in the glass the child
awakens to
his absence. Not what

anyone pre-
dicted—merely what
everyone knows.

3

I keep harking back
to this. Hucking you
a chynik—as my

mother used to say.
But the pot's empty
whatever I say.

There isnt even
the fabulous pot
for pissing in. But

we have to believe
there *is* this. And *this*
is the poetry.

4

I want to get up
and do a dance for
you. Who will never

see—though I am no
dancer—as my wife
will agree. As if

death were my Torah—
as if all my words
beating the rhythm

demanded motion
from this body for
every body.

5

People astonish
me. But I'm crazy.
They always talk as

though they knew something.
Anything but death
creates them. They lie

as casually as
journalists. Look at
the day as though it

were property or
stock. They havent yet
gotten over birth

and never will. But
I'm nuts. Know myself
their ignoramus.

6

We dont want
to know. We
want and that's

what we know.
Live by—live
under. The

seething dis-
covery.
Rock. Child. Stick.

7

You have to
take off your
hat to God

whatever
else you might
care to say

for this—but
with your hat
comes the head.

8

The difficult thing
is to say nothing
and mean it—or more
give it no meaning.

9

The silence you hear
isnt silence.
The death you live through

isnt death. Silence
speaks for itself.
Death for nothing.

10

There's a lot more death
in living
than most of us

surmise or—
when it comes—surmount.
But we are buoyed

by the edge of
the wave—even as
flotsam is.

11

It isn't for want
of something to say—
something to tell you—

something you should know—
but to detain you—
keep you from going—

feeling myself here
as long as *you* are—
as long as you *are*.

12

The train
gone

Distant
instant

Here
you are.

13

As though it
were too good
to be true

And something
(sensing it)
had to give

An apple
apropos
of nothing.

14

It comes to . . . What?
Adding up the days
and then again

subtracting them—
feeling what is lost
accumulate.

15

No one
to answer
the phone

Now the
silence is
ringing.

NINE POEMS

BIAN ZHILIN

Translated from the Chinese by Eugene Eoyang

A BUDDHIST MONK

When day has done tolling its bells, it's another day,
    And a monk dreams a profound and pallid dream:
    Over how many years, shadows and traces are left behind,
In the memory seen only in a glimpse,
In the ruined temple, everywhere a vague scent pervades,
    Lamented bones are left in the censer as of old,
    Along with the sad fate of loyal youths, faithful maidens,
Wearily wriggling through the Buddhist sutras forever.

In a deep stupor, dream-talk foams out at the mouth,
    His head once again faces the skull-like drum,
    His head, the drum, are alike empty and heavy,
One knock after another, mesmerizing mountains and streams,
The mountains and streams slumber indolently in the evening mist,
And once more, he is done tolling the dolorous bell of another day.
(October 1930–January 1931)

A LONG JOURNEY

If one were to follow the thread of the camel's wavelike trail,
  Swelling up in the great slumbering seas of sand,
With a string of bells, tinkling soft and low,
  Piercing through the twilight loneliness,

Then, we'd put up our tents almost anywhere,
  Letting a hard life numb us into a sound sleep,
A large crock with a thick brew, both sour and sweet,
  Would soak into our bodies through and through:

No use worrying if one can see oases in dreams,
  So long as we are dead to the world,
A gale of a wind, swirling around sand and stone, might come
    stealthily
    To bury us, and that would dispose of things neatly.
                    (*October 1930–January 1931*)

OLD TOWN DREAM

There were two kinds of sounds in an old town:
Both desolate:
During the day, it was a fortuneteller's gong,
At night, it was a watchman's rattle.

One can't break up someone else's dream.
The one who dreams is like
A blind man walking along the street,
One step after another.
He knows which cobblestone is low
And which cobblestone high,
And how old the young ladies are in each house.

When one breaks into someone else's dream,
Then dreaming is like

A nightwatchman patrolling the streets,
One step after another.
He knows which cobblestone is low,
Which cobblestone high,
And which houses are shut up tight as a drum.

Third watch, midnight. Listen.
Little Mao's father,
This little boy is crying so much, no one can sleep.
All the time, crying in a dream,
Tomorrow, let's go get his fortune told.

Now, it's deep in the night,
Now, it's a clear, chill afternoon. . . .
The watchman's rattle crosses the bridge,
The fortuneteller's gong also crosses the bridge,
What never stops is the sound of the waters flowing under the bridge.

(*1933*)

AUTUMN WINDOW

Like a middle-aged man,
Turning back to see the footprints of the past:
With one step, a vast desert of sand;
Roused from a confused dream,
Listening to half a sky of evening crows.

Looking at the evening sun against the grayish walls,
Brings to mind a tubercular in the early stages,
Putting up an old mirror to the evening dusk,
Dreaming of the flushed giddiness of youth.

(*October 26, 1933*)

COMPOSITION OF DISTANCES

I think about going up to my study to read a chapter of *The Decline
    and Fall of the Roman Empire,*
When a star, dating from the decline of Rome, appears in the news-
    paper.*
The newspaper falls away. With the atlas open, I think of someone
    far away:
The picture mailed here also shows a scene of vast twilight.
(The star came just at dusk, idle; let's visit a while)
Grayish the sky, grayish the sea, grayish the road.
Where did it come from? I still can't tell by a clod of earth held up
    to the lamp.†
Suddenly, I hear from outside a thousand doors the sound of my
    name.
How tired I am! Is someone toying with my small boat?
My friend brings me a forecast of snow, at five o'clock.

A ROUND TREASURE BOX

I have fantasized that from somewhere (the River of Heaven?)
I fished out a round treasure-box.
It contained several kinds of jewels:
Item: a crystalline drop of mercury,
Reflecting the image of the entire world,

* In the December 26, 1934, edition of the *Da-gong bao,* there was a
dispatch from the London Reuters News Agency: "Two weeks ago, as-
tronomers discovered a new star which appeared in the north. According to
experts, this star has been particularly brilliant these past two days; its
distance is estimated at 1500 light years away from the earth. Therefore, its
explosive death-throes occurred at about the time of the fall of the Roman
Empire. It has taken until now for the light from that conflagration to
reach us."

† The Historical Supplement of the *Da-gong bao* for December 29, 1934,
carried an excerpt from Wang tong-chun's *Kai-fa-ho-tao-ji:* "At night,
running about in the wilderness, I suddenly lost my way: but all I needed
to do was to pick up a handful of earth and I knew where I was."

—Item: torchfire of golden yellow
Enveloping entire a festive feast,
Item: a fresh drop of rain
That holds all of your sighs last night . . .
Don't go to some watch shop,
Listening to your youthful spring being gnawed away by silkworms.
Don't go to some antique store
To buy your grandfather's old knickknacks.
Look at my round treasure-box
And go with me on my drifting boat.
We will go, although those in the cabin
Will be forever in the blue bosom of heaven,
Although your handshake
Will be a bridge. A bridge! But a bridge
Is also built inside my round treasure-box;
So, here's my round treasure-box for you,
Or for them, and perhaps they can just
Wear, pendant on the ears, these items:
A pearl—a precious stone—a star?

                              (*July 8, 1935*)

MIGRATION OF BIRDS

How many courtyards for how many patches of blue sky?
You go and divide them up, I'm leaving.
Let the white doves, bells on their necks, circle overhead three
     times,
But perhaps the camel bells are further off. Listen.
Spin a top to pull you out; fly a kite to drag you along.
Shall I hail the paper hawk, swallow, cock, in threes and fours
To fly up to the sky—to welcome the geese coming from the south?

Furthermore, might we be the playthings of children?
Let us check out a library book on "Migration of Birds."
Well, are you in favor or are you against
The new ordinance against airplanes over the city?
My thoughts are like little spiders riding on trembling gossamer,

Pulling me just enough to lodge me off. I want to leave.
Let's take care of things after we return.
How many courtyards for how many patches of blue sky?
How can I be like a hopeless *radio*
Vainly reaching up with its antenna-arms on the rooftops,
Unable to draw from a distance the sounds I want.

FEVERISH NIGHT

I really have a mind to say: "My heart will race with the clock."

Caught a cold, as twilight goes once again from the east,
Then comes back east, rushing back on two warm legs.
Squandering half a cold in the breezes of late spring:
Why are the eyes red? The nostrils raw?
Could be, lamp, lamp, lamp, you bother me.

In the end everything is lonely. You won't tell anyone, will you?
(At the time, you were drifting off to sleep.)
"Look, love, really, really,
I can't keep your company, with you listening to me snore."
You thought someone was about to ask discreetly,
Not knowing who sent those bouquets of fresh flowers.
You listened, patting dust off shirt and sleeve as you spoke,
"The flowers have bloomed? And I thought it was too early."

The two dilemmas are real: the heart outraces our years,
Then falls behind, by the wayside, by this much:
Those who "understand" say "Sick people think of their parents."
What? It's like a small child calling out for his big brother.
My thought intrudes: "My heart is racing with the clock."

There, there, there, we should be resting.
"Sleep, now, all is hope,
Sleep, now, all is hardship!"

It doesn't matter who sang the lullaby, and for whom.
The watch on the pillow sounds:
"Tick-tick, take your pick." *

A CIGARETTE BUTT

In the midst of banter, a cigarette butt is tossed aside.
I look down, thoughtful at the smoke that trails
Into the distance, toward the horizon—
It disappears—and what about others over the horizon?

This sort of person is muddleheaded,
So, just outside the circle of banter,
By himself, he saves the cigarette butt from the cobblestones,
Not bothering even to hum, "From a vast desert, a lone wisp of
    smoke."

* The original is onomatopoetic: *ying-mian bo-bo;* it also puns on the
cry of a hawker on the street: "Chewy noodles, fine pastries!"

THE FEAST OF ICARUS

SAMUEL HAZO

The poet imitates Icarus. He is inspired to dare impossibility even if this means that he might and probably will fail in the attempt. His fate is to try to find silence's tongue, to say what is beyond saying, to mint from the air he breathes an alphabet that captivates like music. His victory, if it comes at all, must of necessity be a victory of the instant, a lyric split-second of triumph, quick as a kiss. He must live in, see through, and simultaneously rise above. No wonder he has little in common with the historian or the philosopher, who tend to become soberer, even somberer, with age—as if the sheer weight of year after burdening year and the necessity of knowing and understanding and remembering were too much. But the poet concedes in advance to the years and all their baggage their ultimate pindown, their capacity to crush, their parenthesizing amens. Conceding this, he nonetheless wants to transcend the parentheses, as he must, en route. It was the poet in Icarus who dreamed of rising above a sea-level fate that would sadden and weight him down long before it killed him. Feathering his arms, he flew into what couldn't be done. He knew impossibility would down him in the end, but up he went regardless. Why? For the poetry of it. Falling, he had the memory of a new height and no regrets.

I know an architect who designed the tallest all-brick structure in the world. It is a twenty-two story apartment in Pittsburgh, Pennsylvania. When I told him that I had seen brick buildings that were taller than his, he explained that there was a difference between brick buildings where the bricks simply covered a steel superstructure and brick buildings where there was no "steel skeleton" and where the bricks were doing "all the work." In his building, he stressed, the bricks were the primary source of support. I then asked him if twenty-two stories were the maximum height for such structures. His answer was that it was possible to go to forty-four. "Forty-five?" I asked. I was determined to learn the limit. He said that anything beyond forty-four would involve very careful calculations. Then he explained that the maximum height could never really be discovered since most architects as a matter of course as well as a matter of legal obligation kept their "artificial spaces" well below or within the maximum strengths of construction materials to allow for human miscalculation. This ended the conversation, but it left me unsatisfied. Yet, even allowing for human miscalculation, the entire problem struck me as having an Icarian dimension. How high was too high? How much was ever enough? Icarus "solved" the problem of finding his particular mean through experience. His excess preceded his fall, but somewhere in his excessive climb he passed where he should have stopped. But isn't this always the case? You either strike the exact balance (usually by luck) or you go beyond it. Undershooting is no help; that still leaves the mean unknown. Overshooting reveals it by passing it. So Blake was right when he said, "You never know what is enough unless you know what is more than enough."

That we live within restraints is true. That we would like to live without restraints is also true. I am not thinking of people like Coleridge, who wanted to escape all the restrictions of British institutionalism and live unfettered on the banks of the Susquehanna. (Why the Susquehanna? Simply because he liked the sound of the name.) Nor am I thinking of rebellion against oppression or the lure of nudism, which tends to be a warm-weather credo at best. The problem is more subtle than that. What I have in mind are those times when we overstep ourselves without fully understanding how or why what is happening is happening. When, for example, does casual bantering suddenly become anger? When does a passing attraction become the desire to possess? When does dining to satiety become gluttony? If I asked how instead of when, I am sure that the answers to these questions would remain just as elusive. In the history of every person there are instances when he or she no longer tolerated a restraint, resisted what confined or limited, broke through if only to discover that more restraints like more horizons were created by the effort. The restraint could have been anything from a speed limit to the dictates of fashion. Or it could have been reason itself. The impulse to go beyond reason and even to want to live beyond reason is as old as Icarus. Older, in fact. It is as if the promise of life lies not within bounds but beyond bounds, and it is the rare man or woman who has not responded to the summons of that promise for selfish or for the most noble reasons. The passion of Caligula to concentrate in his own person the infinite possibilities of power is an example of the former. As for the latter, I think of what the widowed Ruth in the Old Testament said to her mother-in-law Naomi after Naomi urged her to do the sensible, the reasonable, the natural thing and marry again: "Whithersoever thou shalt go, I will go; and where thou shalt dwell, I also will dwell. Thy people shall be my people, and thy God my God."

Suppression creates resistance. And active resistance against intolerable suppression always summons us to rely on the verbs of ascension to characterize it. Rebellions are thus called uprisings. Guerrillas *mount* attacks against their adversaries. For the rebel, being indomitable means finally not being put down. And rebels and revolutionaries do not rest until they have gained the upper hand. The final victory means the lowering on one flag and the hoisting up of another. Height rhymes with the atmosphere of supremacy and is the antithesis of all that is downtrodden. All this is familiar, even platitudinous, but what is at the basis of this resistance, this unwillingness to acquiesce to subjugation, this arterial no? Politically there are many reasons, but what is common to all is that resistance, or rather the courage to resist, is the child of hatred and fear. It is fear that first fires the rebel-to-be, fear *of* his oppressor, fear *for* himself and those dear to him. This then is replaced by hatred for the individual or group or nation that is the cause of his fear. The two feelings co-exist for a time until the rebel-to-be reaches a point where he begins to hate what he fears more than he fears it. At that instant he becomes a resister and proceeds to find the means to implement his will to resist. Frequently such sagas end in the overthrow of oppressors and are just as frequently followed by excesses of "justice" on the part of the overthrowers. It is inevitable. Hold dry wood under water for a time and then release it quickly, and the wood will rise to the surface with such force that it will go higher than the surface itself before it settles on the sea.

Not the light in the eyes of Romeo when he first glimpsed Juliet in profile nor the new life in Dante's eyes at the sight—his only sight—of Beatrice. Not the look of Monica when she saw Augustine at his worst. Not the slow, still disbelieving stare of Orpheus when he dropped his lyre and saw, at that instant, Eurydice, alive again. Not the blurred softness in the eyes when tears are its final and only possible words as when lovers meet after long separations or know they will never meet again. These are not the eyes of Icarus. Rather the straight gaze of fishermen who spend long periods at helms reading the fish-thick prairies of the Baltic or El Mar Caribe. Or the crow-footed squint of cowboys and hunters. Or the measuring looks of bakers as they bake. Or the quickness in the eyes of athletes, especially baseball players at bat with the ball coming. Or the eyes of operators in control towers monitoring radar. Or the eyes of surgeons in the very act of surgery. Or the eyes of poets when a poem starts and they go with it. Or the eyes of seamstresses. Or the eyes of grooms and brides or all those who choose someone else irrevocably. Or the eyes of women in the final weeks and even hours of pregnancy. Hemingway's eyes. The eyes of Albert Camus. The eyes of pilots as they land and the eyes of those on the ground who watch them land. Picasso's eyes. The eyes of a medieval monk of Bulgaria who carved scenes from the life of Christ in a rosewood diptych the size of a dinner platter in ultramicroscopic detail over a period of a decade, carving every day as long as the light lasted, losing his sight completely on the day the work was finished. The monk is anonymous, but the work remains in a monastery museum near Sofia and speaks for the man who made it at the cost of his eyes, his eyes. For history, epitaph enough, monument enough.

If Icarus means anything, he means that we desire experience, or rather we desire the experience of experience unencumbered by prudence, which implies that we desire the heretofore unexperienced. This comes down to the hankering in us to proceed from what we know to what we don't know, since the desire for experience is usually the desire for the not yet known or at least the desire for the known re-known freshly. To let the body go on where only the imagination has had the courage to venture, that is the lure. To let the mind catch up later, as it invariably does, sorting, justifying, rejecting, remembering, that is the consequence. Experience is thus not knowledge. It is simply experience. It is what occupies us totally at the present. Its fruit is awareness. Granted, experience that is never thought about is never completely or partially understood. Thus experience in this sense has us rather than vice versa. Granted, the romantic is he or she who hungers for experience without grasping what experience teaches so that life for the romantic is but a sequence of episodes in subsequences. Granted as well that experience does not fill us with understanding simply because it happened to us. We must think about it. And it is this thinking that creates a knowledge that derives from perspective, and it is this knowledge that is the prelude to understanding and the dry, tough eucharist of wisdom. But this comes later. And the Icarus in us is not concerned with later. He is too busy obeying the body's imperative, which wants the fullest awareness and satisfaction right now. The mind's primary impulse is to adjudicate this awareness and measure this satisfaction, to make sense even where there may be no sense. And we are poised between the two and are compelled to live with the tension. We yearn for experience without responsibility, but the need to come to terms with it is ineluctable. What is usually sacrificed in the effort to come to terms is the spontaneity of the experience as and when it happened. It is reminiscent of the spontaneity that is destroyed when the intimate is made public. It loses in mystery what it gains in notice as is the case with whispers, nudism, or sexual intercourse. But the mind is oblivious. Mystery is its enemy because mystery leaves it in suspense. Vexed, it is unable to judge and unwilling to acknowledge that the mystery of life even in the face of sheer absurdity is often what life really is. No matter. Icarus is there to remind us that the yet to be experienced moment waits only for the experiencer regardless of consequence. That is his invitation. He asks us to enter the moment.

TWO POEMS

EDWIN BROCK

LANDFALL

Snapshots may help: the hard white
light of south coast holidays;
stretched breasts in a boned bra
and my own belly held in.

But these stained papers have
no memory, no pain. And that,
perhaps, is pain itself.

Maps may help: tomorrow will be
cold with periods of bright sunshine;
only we do not remember what the man
said yesterday about today

nor that looking back is as impossible
as looking this way was then.

After evensong at evening college,
catching up, trying to understand
the phenomenon of choice

as though we were ever free
to choose or would recognize
the moment when it came.

Wanting to know this place
yet not knowing what we came to do
nor how the debris of all those others
ever belonged to us.

Now there is no landscape, we
listen. Or, rather, hear a part of it
as though they want it for ourselves.

And, using a style to make a place to
go from, find those snapshots are no help.

I have not seen you for a long time.
Nor you, nor you. I have not been
here for a long time myself.

There is no hurry. Tomorrow will be
cold with periods of bright sunshine

and this may be the moment
that is trying to begin.

MORNING FLIGHT

The mad are always moving:
not on, back, up or down
but like those surrealist toys
which move because to stop
would end the joke.

From my nine o'clock bus
the Health Service junkie
clutches his jacket and
runs into traffic. I
check my watch obsessively:
"You'll get St. Vitus Dance
if you fidget like that!"
my mother says, her mouth
a shout of perpetual motion.

Hour after hour I keep my body
still, trained to attention,
its noise disciplined inside:
fingernails are a small price
to pay for survival.

Once, perhaps twice, at the end
of music. . . . No, not even then.
Not in love nor in prayer
but knowing that birth can come only
from death's closest approximation.

HISTORIES

ROBERT LAX

Edited by Robert Butman

the man
& his whole family
looked like
clean bottles
into which
life had been poured
pure & shining

he sat
on the edge of his bed
all night

day came
& he continued to sit there

he thought he would never be able
to understand
what had happened

had they invented
nothing
in the west

no single gesture?

the old cat
knew the barn
better
than anyone else

and always had
her litter
in a different
part
of it

tosca's father
would only let her
perform once a year
& at a good price

the rest of the time
she spent practicing
flips
on a slack-wire
out in the yard

i wish i'd married
some man
who'd owned a department store
instead of you

you know why?

because then
i'd have all the things i wanted
not some
daisy
you found in the field

allowed
the sun to dry her nails
as though
it had
no other work
in the world

otto & wanda's
only
real life
was in bed

outside
they went through the motions

attending concerts
& openings
at the museum

but nothing
they saw or heard
really impressed them

when i play house
i don't play
either the poppa
or the mamma

it's me
as though i was playing
i was
the house

put another record
on the gramophone
Auntie

Sophie
here
says
she wants
to shake

mrs. sims'
only bit of equipment

was a kind of inner feeling
that would follow her along
to parties
assert itself
on shopping tours
tell her
which beggars
were good
& which
undeserving

when she met someone
she felt
she was meant
to meet him

much as the sun
was meant
to shine by day
and the moon by night

when she was disappointed
she felt that this was intended, too

a lesson lying in wait for her
since before the beginning of time

said he'd rather
stay around
a hundred years
as a man

than a thousand years
as a poem

but sometimes
I think
he was kidding

the angel came to him & said

I'm sorry, mac, but
we talked it over
in Heaven
& you're going

to have to live
a thousand years

fleetfooted emma kropotkin
was faster
than anyone thought
she lifted more hats
from department stores
than most other customers
bought

her daughter gertrude
was studying
to be
a bridesmaid
and was continually
dressed

in light blue
tulle

put
every
cent
he had
into
Amer-
i-
can
Revol-
ving
Door

ERNEST'S MOTHER

ABELARDO CASTILLO

Translated from the Spanish by Gregory Woodruff

Whether or not Ernest ever found out that she had come back (and how she had come back) I never discovered, but the fact is that soon afterward he went away to Tala to live, and that whole summer long we saw him only once or twice. It was hard to look him in the face. It was as if the idea Julio had put into our minds—for it was his idea, Julio's, and it was a strange idea, disturbing and dirty—made us feel guilty. Not that we were puritans. At that age, and in a place like that, nobody is a puritan. But just for that reason, because there was nothing pure or God-fearing about us and all in all we were pretty much like everyone else, there was something disturbing about the idea. Something inadmissible, cruel. Seductive. Above all, seductive.

It was a long time ago. The Alabama was still standing, that building just outside of town, on the main road. The Alabama was an inoffensive kind of restaurant, inoffensive by day at least, because after eleven at night it turned into a sort of primitive night club. It ceased to be primitive when the Turk got the idea of adding some rooms on the ground floor and bringing in women. One woman he did bring.

"No!"

"Yes. A woman."

"Where did he find her?"

Julio put on that mysterious manner that we knew so well—because he had mastered a special repertory of gestures, phrases, and inflections which set him oddly apart, and which we envied: a small-town, moderately priced Beau Brummel—and asked, in a low voice:

"Where is Ernest now?"

In the country, I told him. From time to time Ernest would go to spend a few weeks in the cabin at Tala. This had been going on ever since his father—after that business with his wife—had refused to come back to the town. I said, in the country, and then asked:

"What has Ernest to do with it?"

Julio took out a cigarette. He smiled.

"Do you know who the woman is that the Turk brought in?"

Anibal and I glanced at each other. Now I remembered Ernest's mother. Nobody spoke. She had gone off four years earlier, with one of those theatrical troupes that tour the provinces: "A brazen hussy," my grandmother had remarked at the time. A pretty woman. Dark, with a full figure: I remembered. And she couldn't be too old, maybe about forty.

"Going pretty far, isn't it?"

There was a silence, and it was then that a look from Julio planted the idea in our minds. Or very likely we'd already thought of it.

"If she weren't his mother . . ."

That was all he said.

Who knows. Perhaps, then, Ernest found out sometime that summer, we saw him only a couple of times (later, they said, his father sold everything, and they were never heard from again), and the few times we did see him, it was hard to look him in the face.

"Guilty of what? After all, the woman is public property, and she's been at the Alabama for half a year now. If we wait for the Turk to bring another, we'll die of old age."

And he added, Julio that is, that all we had to do was get hold of a car, go, pay—it could all be done in no time—and that if we hadn't the nerve to go with him he'd find someone who wasn't just a baby in long pants, and Anibal and I weren't going to let anyone talk to us like that.

"But it's his mother."

"His mother! What do you mean by mother? A sow's the mother of a litter, isn't she?"

"And she eats up the piglets."

"Of course she eats them. What about it?"

"There's this about it. Ernest grew up with us."

I said something about the times we had played together; that got me thinking, and somebody voiced aloud the very thought that had occurred to me. It may have been I myself:

"Remember what she was like?"

Of course we remembered. For months now we'd been remembering: she was dark, with a full figure; nothing motherly about her.

"Besides, half the town has already been up there. We're the only ones."

We're the only ones. The argument had the force of a provocation, and the very fact of her returning was another provocation. Well, disgustingly, everything seemed easier. I believe now—possibly—that if it had been any other woman, perhaps we shouldn't have seriously considered going. Possibly. We were a bit afraid to say so but, secretly, we were on Julio's side, helping him to convince us: because the equivocal, the inadmissible, the monstrously seductive aspect of the whole affair was, perhaps, that the mother of one of us was involved.

"Don't talk filth, please," said Anibal to me.

A week later Julio assured us he'd be able to get hold of the car that very night. Anibal and I waited for him on the boulevard.

"Probably he backed out."

"Or they wouldn't let him have the car."

I said it contemptuously, I remember perfectly. And yet it was a kind of prayer: probably he backed out. Anibal's voice was strained, trying to sound indifferent:

"I'm not going to wait around all night; if he doesn't come in ten minutes, I'm leaving."

"I wonder what she's like now."

"Who . . . her?"

He'd been on the point of saying, his mother. I could tell by his face. But he said, her. Ten minutes is a long time, and it was hard to forget now the time when we'd gone to play with Ernest, and she, the dark, full-blown woman, had asked if we'd like to stay and have a glass of milk. The dark woman. Full-blown.

"Sickening business, eh?"

"You're scared," I told him.

"No, not scared; it's something else."

I shrugged my shoulders.

"As a rule, women have children. She was bound to be somebody's mother."

"It's not the same thing. We know Ernest."

I said that wasn't the worst of it. Ten minutes. The worst of it was that she knew us, that she would be looking at us. Yes, she would. I don't know why, but I was certain of one thing: when she looked at us, something was going to happen.

Anibal had a frightened look now, and ten minutes is a long time. He asked:

"And if she throws us out?"

I was about to answer when my stomach doubled up in a knot: an automobile was roaring down the main street, mowing down the minutes, the exhaust wide open.

"Julio," we exclaimed, with one voice.

The car swung round in a powerful curve. Everything about it was powerful: the headlights, the horn, the exhaust. It gave us courage. The bottle he had brought gave us courage too.

"I stole it from the old man."

His eyes were glittering. So were ours, Anibal's and mine, after the first swallows. We turned down Paraiso, headed toward the railway crossing. Her eyes had glittered, too, when we were kids, or perhaps it only seemed to me now that I had seen them glittering. And she had worn make-up, lots of make-up. Especially on her mouth.

"She smoked, do you remember?"

We were all of us thinking the same thing, but I was not the one who said that, it was Anibal; what I said was that yes, I remembered, and I added that you have to begin some way or other.

"How much longer?"

"Ten minutes."

And once again it was a long ten minutes; but now they were long the other way round. I can't explain. Perhaps it was because I was recalling, all of us were recalling, that afternoon when she was cleaning the floor, and it was summer, and her dress slipped away from her body as she bent down, and we had nudged each other.

Julio pressed down on the throttle.

"After all, it's a punishment"—but your voice carried no conviction, Anibal—"a revenge in Ernest's name, it'll teach her . . .

"A punishment, the hell you say!"

Somebody—I think I was the one—came out with a really vile obscenity. I'm sure I was the one. The three of us were roaring with laughter, and Julio put on more speed.

"And if she has us thrown out?"

"Are you sick in the head? If she gets on her high horse and tries to make trouble, I'll speak to the Turk, or I'll raise such a row they'll close the joint for not giving the customers decent service."

At that hour there were few people in the bar: a traveler or so, two or three truck drivers; from the town, nobody at all. And, heaven knows why, that made me feel bolder. Immune. I winked at the blonde behind the counter; Julio, in the meantime, was talking to the Turk. The Turk looked at us, as though sizing us up, and I could tell from the defiant look on Anibal's face that he was feeling his oats too. The Turk said to the little blonde:

"Take them upstairs."

The blonde climbing the stairs: I can remember her legs. And the way her hips swayed. I remember saying something indecent, and the girl's replying in kind: something that (maybe on account of the cognac we'd had in the automobile, or the gin we'd had at the bar) struck us as terribly funny. And then we were in a tidy room, impersonal, almost like a study, with a little table: it could have been a dentist's waiting room. I thought, maybe they're going to pull our teeth. I said so to the other two:

"Maybe they're going to pull our teeth."

It was impossible to smother our laughter entirely, but we tried to make as little noise as we could. We spoke very low.

"As though we were at Mass," said Julio, and once again this seemed singularly amusing; but the funniest moment of all was when Anibal, covering his mouth and inhaling noisily, said:

"Just wait and see if the priest doesn't come out in a minute."

My stomach ached, and my throat was parched from laughing so hard. But all of a sudden we turned serious. The man who had been inside came out. A short, chubby man, with something piggish about him. A satisfied pig. Jerking his head back toward the room, he made a face, rolled up his eyes, and licked his lips. It was sickening to watch.

And then, as we heard the man's footsteps going down the stairs, Julio asked:

"Who'll go first?"

We looked at each other. Until this moment it hadn't occurred to me—or I hadn't let it occur to me—that we were going to be alone, separated—that was the thing, separated—before her. I shrugged.

"I don't know. Any of us."

Through the half-opened door we could hear the sound of water running from a tap. The lavatory. Then silence, and a light that struck us in the face: the door had just been opened wide. There she stood. And we stared at her, spellbound. The wrapper hanging loose, half opened, and that summer afternoon long ago, when she was still Ernest's mother, and the dress slipped away from her body, and she asked us if we'd stay for a glass of milk. Only now the woman was blonde. Blonde and full-blown. Smiling with a professional smile, a smile that was somehow vicious.

"Well?"

Her voice, unexpectedly, startled me: it was the same voice. Yet something had changed in her, and in the voice. The woman smiled again and said again "Well?"; and it was like an order, a hot, sticky command. Perhaps it was this quality in it that brought all three of us to our feet. Her wrapper, I recall, was dark, almost transparent.

"I'll go," muttered Julio, and stepped resolutely forward.

He took two steps: two, and that was all. Because then she looked us full in the face and, abruptly, he stopped. Why, we don't know: fear, guilt perhaps, or disgust. And that's where it ended. Because she was looking at us, and I knew already that when she looked at us something would happen. The three of us stopped motionless, frozen in our tracks; and as she watched us, staggering, God knows what our faces looked like, her own face slowly, gradually, took on a strange aspect, fearful to look upon. Because at first, for a few seconds, all it revealed was perplexity, a failure to understand; but after that, no. After that, it was as though she had heard something, darkly, and she looked at us in fear, stricken, questioning. It was only then that she spoke. She asked if anything had happened to him, to Ernest.

She closed the wrapper across her breast as she asked us.

WHY AM I ALWAYS ASKING

DORA GABE

Translated from the Bulgarian by Jascha Kessler and Alexander Shurbanov

1
Grant me,
O Life!
the least kernel
of a soul
on earth—
that I may give away
what grows
from you,
my heart's
warmth.

2
When we were children
our oaks
touched the clouds—
and their long shadows
covered our village.

Where are they now?
In dream?
In memory?
Did Time take them,
chasing after
us?

3
A bird perches
outside my window,
and darts two beady eyes at me.
What's it waiting for?
Can
I guess
the secret of her silence,
or
will I
be powerless
before it?

4
It's life
I feel
whirling round me.
Sounds,
tones all pass,
fading,
leaving me
once more
to my fate.
Will it bring me
to the end,
or come
trailing after?

5

Giving me birth,
my mother
saw
her star
against a pure sky.
But whom
did she give
her blessing to,
to keep me
from being
her fate?!

6

The seeds buried themselves
deep
to keep
the wind from blowing them away
before they could take up
the force of life.
Did the white snowdrop
hurry
over the snow,
to welcome
life
with its chastity?

7

In the tunnel's twilight
trickles
threaded the walls,
and some transparent
yet living blade
of clear grass
sprouted from the water,
two tiny leaves
on a frail stalk.

And this, O Life,
is where you're born?
Unafraid of solitude?

8
Frightened,
I fled
the dark forest!
Do trees always grow
in silence?
Will the huge-winged
Eagle
sleep in the
stillness?
But I don't wish,
I don't care to be a
She-eagle.
Keep me, Life,
in your heart!

9
All space
Split by a little
bird,
startling the stillness.
Oh breath
of the very earth!
Did you give her
birth?

10
Still on and on . . .
where's an end to it?
Why am I always asking,
don't I know nothing

ends?
What answer
do I wait for—
and from whom?

11
O Earth!
How can I
count
all the laws,
yet go on living
lawfully?

12
When I woke,
the sun looked in on me
through a clear pane.
I asked,
"Are you shining for me?"
No reply.
Then I asked you,
though I see you not,
though I know you not,
though you are not . . .

13
I understood you as well,
ah, Vitality—
I could feel my self
in you
insatiable now
to deliver
the life of the earth.

14
Why am I always asking?
They stuffed
my heart
with answers.
Why?
Why perturb
me?
Answer them,
little ladybug
sitting on my finger—
but why have you spread
your tiny wings
and flown away?

15
Now I meet
my life's ending.
I'm giving it all away
and making no more mistakes.
Yet what other world
will take me
with an empty
soul?

CHILD OF THE LIGHT

with a note on the use of the word *absorption*

BETSY ADAMS

To Hiroishi Mizukami

A note on the use of the word *absorption* (Absorption and *a*bsorption used in poem)

It has to be pointed out that use of the word absorption by the physical scientist is limited to a specific meaning: the excitation of electrons in matter when that matter absorbs a specific wavelength (frequency) of light. In the body of the poem, Absorption will be used when referring to this interaction of light with matter.

The use of the word absorption in the health professions and in areas of the biological sciences dealing with consumption of food materials from which organisms derive their energy necessary for life processes will hereafter be written *a*bsorption, to distinguish it from the physical scientist's usage.

The only living organisms capable of carrying on both Absorption and *a*bsorption are the photosynthetic bacteria and the photosynthetic plants, which possess specialized chemical molecules capable of entrapping light directly.

Ultimately, the source of ALL chemically utilizable energy on this earth for biologically living organisms comes from these photosynthetic organisms. We humans just *a*bsorb, we can no longer Absorb (except for the vitamin-D production by our skin when UV

light is Absorbed from our sun . . . a relatively trivial process by
comparison with those occurring all about us in the universe).

Part I

1
Encapsuled: black bundle tossed about within the sheaves of light.
Torrents surround the hide of itself, lifted and swayed. Always
sucking, sucking upon the sheaves. Faceless, voiceless, eyeless.
Torrents within the casing feed upon the light. Blasphemous, in
black, irregular opacities. Protrusions of itself into the paths of light.
Clamorous, with miniscule blind focii upon each point as it enters,
contacts the sloping sides of the sheaves of light.

2
Wait here, then. See the blisters of light exploding before their
eventual destruction into a hollow, irregular thing. Crafty, no.
Stotted, no. But lingers. Within the space alloted by the sheaves,
which sway as branches sway in moonlight or in sun. Sway. And
move in eddying paths about the rotted, gutted things which feed
upon the light. Gluttonous, yes. Rapacious, yes. Round, opaque
bundled dead birth itself, thrown upon the waves.

3
From where?: Mercurial forces, no. Weathering forces, no.
Measurable forces. Never. None but those of interactions which
occur between absorption and that which is being Absorbed. Craven,
yes. Multitudinous, yes. Wretched, yes. Above all else the bundle
is a wretched, one-time, and timed thing.

4
Severance impossible: light bears upon itself all movement of the

births from itself. From that time eons ago when the first absorption occurred: when mouths opened, and feeding, in deep seas upon base molecular structures encompassed these first definitive, and now, diverging lines.

No longer enough room for only the light. But life, itself, has begun. And in its beginning, rapacious black holes have trundled themselves upon the wake of the light. Meet. And would meld. Would attempt the fusion. But will never succeed. Never. Until each individual death is accomplished.

Part II

1

What fascinates us most are the spicules which align the sides of the black tumbling and trundled thing. Which afford us focus for interactions among sheaves and the black rapacious thing, itself.

2

If I were to birth you, it would be a face. Tumultuous, wretched, and lying bound in black as light persuaded all about it. Small faces would appear in all your pores as light dribbled inward, and then would as quickly disappear as the light passed through. As it must. For light belongs to no one.

3

Bilious: The color red grows in stems from the sides of the branched limbs purported to be supportive to the black trundled lifelessness. Brought to you, here, and laid upon your doorstep. What will you do today? And tomorrow? For the sheaves of light are nought but the passage these 3.5 billion years that sever you from yourself: Relief immense. Predictable.

4

But, back to the spicules: I deem my face tractable, tradable. I do
not believe in the Japanese proverb that by the age of 40, each of
us is responsible for his/her face.

Forage along the beams of light. Or among them. The sequencial
ruin you will find is black iris on stems which move passively
among brilliant accolades of soundless brilliant receding. I mean,
that light has no meaning for you, for you are called the living.
And you are, by that living, a dead birth.

Part III

1

I see you there. Tossed as I am tossed among the grasping absorp-
tions of ourselves . . mongerers of a light we do not know, and
which we understand even less. Given instruments which turn the
passing of light into miraculous numbers. Which by their own
account, deal not at all with the living.

I abide by the rules of numbers, and by the great consequential
sequences they render absolute: based on axiom of the human eye.
Thus am I trundled. A passenger in the light of light: A focusing
on myriad changing faces which I cast within the sheaves them-
selves. And which, before all, have no recognition of me upon
approach. No understanding of me upon interaction. And no re-
membrance of me upon passing.

2

Black, semisolid thing I am, suspended here. Resounding voice
which reaching back to my own ears, knows no light. Knows noth-
ing of any truth outside the spicules of my faces . . rising, rising,

there, Finally, climactically touching upon one side of the racing
sheave, which in its utter incapacity for knowing, now recedes from
me. And merges, just as unknowingly, into the massively mounded,
tumultuous sheaves of light which lie ahead, behind, Forever,
there.

Part IV

1

Release is possible only when you give up blandishment of your
face: When the receptacles: distortive/replenishing; reverential/
multitudinously rapacious give up themselves, resort to facelessness.
Then and only then will you touch the light.

Quivering clutches of a black marauding (and miraging) hand,
tremulously touching a passing sheave is meaningless: Time will
occlude your senses, will press sperm/ova upon you; will measure
the tred of your black cloaking on the faces of clocks.

2

Let there be no miracles, for they are not necessary. All that is, is
receptiveness to light . . whether from a moon, and hence reflected
light only, but true to itself; or from a sun, second in passing light
exploding in the universe about us.

Be only a human who treds upon the dark path: Who allows the
faces of yourself to reflect emittent light from stars. Who accepts,
and therefore is, trundled surfaces of points which press against the
sheaves, starving. And finding sustenance only in impersonal, real,
death of yourself.

Part V

1
There are thus three words:

Severance/mortgages/release: Severance and release are not the
same. To sever is to give up responsibility to your face before the
time of interactions with the light are finished. Release is that time
when your job is finally, and with peace, completed (is this why
suicide is wrong?). Mortgages are those massive unresolved areas
between you and the interactions: i.e., that you have been given
light. What have you done about it? You owe it to the light/ . .
And always, the great bull rises up from his haunches and demands
at this point: but do I/and Why?

2
As each wave of light which streams, the voices colliding, reeking,
and bending among themselves: What the hell do I owe to any-
body. Face or faceless will I lie down, and I will munch the clover,
the flowers with red wilting heads bleeding and rushing down the
great cuff of fur which lies beneath my neck.

3
I am the bull who blocks the walls from themselves, and from
interactions with themselves and the light. I am the bull who lies
down in the vast mown lawn and gazes far out into the acres, who
leaves never, but basks in the abounded light of a known sun,
moon, stars.

The temperatures will drop to below negative 20, but you will find
me here, the grazer, who has all in this life . . and among all the
faces of myself, owed to me from the sheaves

which, bearing right or left, or nought at all . . and from high
above, I wait for the message to be sent. Graze then, in seeming
faceless, oblivious knowledge, on all the reflected blossoms about me.

4

It is time, then, to bury the envelope. Permanently. And to use the head of the falsely drawn wolf who slavers, as a stake. Time to leave this rotting place which is myself: A Snowqueen. Dead. Who will take none: Absolutely no responsibility for the faces I have borne.

My Snowqueen. My ravenous Bullock, there is not much time/light, left. For you.

Part VI

1

Thus, the interactions of light upon ridges, borders. Upon the tallest reaches of spicules which lie within the trundled borders of the self.

Thus, the faces, which reach out to know the searing cold whiteness which passes, glances and relieved within the mounting light which lies before.

The access I have is the tubules: the tapering, foundering sources of myself, which lie within tapering bundles of movements, gellied and jelly of membranes, the brain, among tormented and bound atoms.

There is no such thing, down here, as a mountain top. There is no such thing, among the ravenous movements of atoms which are my life and my faces, as mountain top.

There is only the brief glancing light as it rushes atop the minute spicules which rise above this valley in which I now lie . . upon my back, waiting. Face, my own, face at the bottom of the world.

2

Dress in black: give yourself the tool to climb up, up and free of
this valley. What you will find are blatant shearing peaks which
level only when the light interacts with them . . which know no
life as you know it. Which abound with a universe in a cold way
you will never wish to know as long as you cling to face.

There is no such thing, here, as a face meeting your own which has
upon it the marks of tendrils of light weeping in from tops of peaks
of the valley; which has marks in blossoming extremities, and
thumbless hands decrying those of faces who would mount the hills
to reach for light.

You must turn to numbers. And then to the fourth level, which is
language, if you would survive as this particular piece of inter-
related matter and small scinters of light. You must be content with
this, no matter how primitive and based in blackness: which is this
side . . away from beloved sheaves of light.

Part VII

the bush, seen:

This morning I went into the fields of the ten acres
and I looked again at the bush which is the border
between myself and the light. And beyond which, she,
herself, has passed.

And I noticed, consciously I suspect,
for the very first time how the branches
which reach from the soil are grey and white;
how the subbranches are red, with red round berries atop.

It is a rosebush, a wild one. Which grows because
the light has planted it there. And which I will someday
be able to pass by as my gate out into the reaches of light.
But today, in the sunlight of the earth and of my own time
upon the earth. The berries were red. Heavy. And red,

And I did not realize that I had gasped. My hand was
on my own throat. My mittens were frozen. The light
which I could see was the red light . . . the opacities
of the most deeply embedded branches smokey, fogged over
as they rended into the great passing sheaves of light.

On the other side: I cannot be there. I am here,
with a small hand and with beasts who pass the light
from startled eyes they wish to share with me.
I am here. And the bodies which are dusky and which
have been buried by me at the side of the house,
Wait. For it is all that we can do.

THE TWELVE HEALERS AND
OTHER REMEDIES

DAVID ZANE MAIROWITZ

Today I received my copy of *The Twelve Healers and Other Remedies* by Edward Bach, M.B., B.S., M.R.C.S., L.R.C.P., D.P.H., along with his thirty-eight little bottles of herbal liquids which "are blest above others in their work of mercy . . . and have been given the power to heal all types of illness and suffering."

The package comes from an address in Muswell Hill, North London, a height from which you can look down on the flatter part of the city, a green place where you can hide out when things down below begin to sicken. If Dr. Bach himself (now deceased) ever hung out up there, with its parks and gardens, I can see how it might inspire him to cure people with flower essences. Here's his wisdom: "This system of healing, which has been Divinely revealed unto us, shows that it is our fears, our cares, our anxieties, and such like that open the path to the invasion of illness. Thus by treating our fears, our cares, our worries, and so on, we not only free ourselves from our illness, but the Herbs given unto us by the Grace of the Creator of all, in addition take away our fears and worries, and leave us happier and better in ourselves." You can find out such things up in happy Muswell Hill because misery, like mine, can't afford to live there.

This box of remedies has taken three weeks to get down the hill to my place. It can't be more than three miles, and there have been no strikes this month at the post office. If Dr. Bach himself were alive, rather than his heirs and devotees, he would have recognized the urgency of my case, probably even sent them round by messenger. I pleaded with them not to delay, even sending more than the £ 4.50 required. This special sloth, you see, which grows under conditions of gray light in this country, now reproduces itself like cancer cells; but the worst is that we don't die of it, only grieve.

For my lingering impatience I have immediately mixed a few drops of a remedy called Impatiens with water, as well as three more of Chestnut Bud. I've switched on my electric heater, cramped myself up in my armchair, and wait to be healed.

I ought to be cold now that the electric heater has stopped. I really should begin to worry that there are no more coins for the meter. If I stopped to consider the coming weekend, the closing of all places of business, the difficulty of finding the right coins to buy my warmth with, the subsequent and inevitable dampness in my bones, the chore of finding a new doctor who would put me on his list (now that the others have rejected me), all this and the need to go into the street, the dismal steps into our freezing summer rain—all this should put me in a rage. But the model of patience I have suddenly become since I fell asleep can laugh at all that.

Before I was healed I never gave myself time to reflect. Moving from distress to distress, all I could hope for were brief moments of calm before the rush of fresh catastrophe. This has been going on now for as long as I can remember, ceaseless unrest, broken only by my few months of faith-healing and brief spell of acupuncture, both of which only slowed me down temporarily.

Now everything has ground to a pace of careful consideration. Instead of forcing things, constantly raging and banging my head against the infuriating closed doors of English life, I am learning how to wait.

To prevent this mood from reaching a pitch of apathy, I coat my tongue with some few drops of Clematis and Wild Rose.

I'm getting nowhere fast. I've moved out of my armchair and thought I'd have a look at the day. The iron bars over my basement window only allow me to see casual footwork up above. No matter how far I crane my neck there is no sky to be seen. The quality of the light in our climate tells me nothing about the hour of the day, and I have recently smashed my watch in one of my rages before I was cured. If this were a city of human scale I would hear some village church chiming the hour or the inevitable whistle of the last train to somewhere else, always on time, speeding away in the night. I have lived in places of such simple precision; and yet, when I did, it was never necessary to tell the time.

I've tried to cook myself a meal, but fumbled it. These eggs were old when they came out of the chicken, if indeed they ever saw the inside of any living thing. Bread stales the moment it leaves the oven and touches the English atmosphere. I crave some black-berries and cream, but the city has shut down for the weekend. Only the Pakistani shops remain open, but I don't want to encour-age them with my money. For their own good.

Anyway, I'm revolted by the thought of food. Dr. Bach, I see, has no remedy for food revulsion, which is discouraging because I'm actually very hungry indeed. I'll try some of his Elm and a bit of Gentian for my discouragement.

In the darker hours comes a disturbance on the stair. I know its footwork. It knocks. Receiving no reply it fumbles beneath a fa-miliar loosened brick for a familiar key and admits itself, knowing without doubt that I am inside.

Jessamy carries her Mitsubishi portable tape recorder as always and immediately advances upon me with the spools already wind-ing out her personal history; indeed, I think she's recorded her knocking and the key in the lock too just to prove, for posterity, that on this occasion I did not open the door for her. This is yet another tape she'll have to transcribe and edit down, then revise so that the facts conform to her desires, all to make up her ever-unfolding, multivolume autobiography in which I, alas, am cast in a supporting role. I have not dared to survive this experience for three weeks now, and here it bursts in upon my rest, will I, nill I.

Because she is in mid-tape Jessamy will not stop for the breath allowed by small talk, even to ask why I have ripped the telephone from the wall or barred her entry by various schemes these three weeks. I didn't want to see her again until Dr. Bach's remedies could prepare me for her, could intervene in this endless exchange of miseries which passes as our life together. Now I have, if not an advocate, at least an ally. When Jessamy rises to her usual brainlessnesses, I can call on the "twelve healers and other remedies" for quick doses of toleration.

Without my consent she is telling about her last night's dream. I don't really care to hear, but Jessamy's dreams create her waking days, causing her to shiver with terror or shimmy with delight, and I had always better listen to them carefully or prepare for shafts of fire and wrath: Several men are chasing her with explicitly carnal intentions. She manages to evade them, but with ever-decreasing will power, while she herself increases in body heat. Suddenly she finds herself transported by this heat back to our French summer island and finds there the traveling family of circus artistes, Variétés Toulousiennes, complete with Gilberto le Jongleur, Anita l'Anthropodiste, and the others who form an important part of our mutual memory.

"I don't want to hear about Gilberto."

"He comes into my dream."

"I'm erasing him from my memory."

"Stuff your memory! This is my dream!"

And so it is. But Jessamy knows how the thought of that summer oppresses me now, and I begin to see that this dream of hers may be a conjured one, designed to strike me with poisonous darts in vulnerable places. It is some kind of revenge for shutting her out of my house and, while seeming to relate an innocent dream, she is really playing at being a sorcerer's apprentice who can fabricate illusions by staring into mirrors for hours on end. I'd better check out Dr. Bach. Honeysuckle: "those who live much in the past, perhaps a time of great happiness. . . . They do not expect further happiness such as they have had."

Jessamy doesn't want any Honeysuckle drops and promptly smacks the bottle from my hand, spilling the contents all over the floor.

"I don't want your stupid drops! I don't want to forget!"

She's screaming again.

"You do Dr. Bach an injury."

"Stuff Dr. Bach, whoever he is. He's my enemy if he makes me forget."

"He can cure you of your obsession with this memory."

"I don't need to be cured! It's a joyful memory!"

Holly: "for the different forms of vexation."

"What poison are you putting in your mouth now?"

"Holly."

I might have answered with a shoe neatly planted in her face, but the remedy has slowed the spiraling rush of my ire. A few more drops do the trick. Besides, such a kick in the teeth would have been recorded on her Mitsubishi, and then what of my reputation when the appropriate volume appears in print?

"I'm telling you my dream!"

I'd better listen or there'll be no peace.

"Gilberto was the last obstacle, with his long Gypsy face that doesn't dare smile because it would break his concentration and force him to drop his juggling pins. He leads me behind the circus tent. All this, I think, comes from something you actually said about Anita . . ."

Oh, not Anita l'Anthropodiste. No. She severs my limbs with each mention of that circus troupe.

"While she was on her back, twirling a huge cylinder with her feet, you wondered out loud what it would be like to make love to her in that position."

"Well?"

"So it was with Gilberto and me. In the dream, he begins to toss his juggling pins in the air, ten, twelve, fifteen at a time, all the while thrusting at me . . ."

"And catches his pins while thrusting . . ."

"Yes. And I'm so intrigued by his act, that I hardly notice him breaking through to me . . ."

"And so?"

". . . and I keep worrying: how can I keep my eyes on Gilberto's amazing juggling and remain faithful to you at the same time?"

"At least it wasn't the Russian dog who jumps through rings of fire."

"I looked for you everywhere in the crowd, but you'd left me alone. You should have been there to break it up!"

Can I have heard correctly? Yes, it's true. Jessamy is kicking my shins, crying, and blaming me for not appearing in her dream. Should I say I was delayed by one of my own? Or should I not add my weight to the mental imbalance of her rage?

"Why didn't you come?!"

"I'm no match for Gilberto."

That seems the right thing to have said, under the demented circumstances, but it only inflames her. I've got my eye on the Mitsubishi "stop" button.

"It was tough not being unfaithful these three weeks. With Gilberto it was touch and go."

"But that was just a dream."

This is not an argument to use on Jessamy. I know it, even as I speak it.

"If Gilberto can just appear to me like that whenever he wants, invading my sleep, he can do anything he likes with me, and you'll be responsible."

What she doesn't seem to understand is that I really don't care to whom she yields up her dubious treasure, whether it be some phantom dream-lover like Gilberto or the milkman of reality. This "dream" of hers is a way of alerting me to an imminent infidelity she wants me to believe is somehow a threat. In this, she's trying to prove it is worth some massive effort to remain together, and that this requires sorcery, phantoms, elaborations of danger and inventions of risk.

I'm for cure.

I often think about winding the Mitsubishi cord around Jessamy's throat and recording her gurgles as she finishes off her autobiography. She seems to be unaware of this because she persists in reminding me of our summer island, of Variétés Toulousiennes, and of some nonsensical promise I made to marry her at the very moment Gilberto le Jongleur was pushing his body miraculously through tight steel hoops. Dr. Bach, I see, has no potion for murderous instincts, but there is a drop of Aspen for moments when "the patient may be terrified of something terrible going to happen, he knows not what."

Jessamy says she wants to stay the night. I wasn't even aware that night had dropped. I no longer look nervously at the window to see what's going on, now I've found contentment. This is thanks to Dr. Bach, and I'll go forward with him now. Every hour of my life has brought some small illness to my surface, never enough to kill or lame me, only to depress me with fevers and lumps. Dr. Bach has shown me that this is only my mind using my body as a dumping ground, and I'll use his "twelve healers and other remedies" to root out the disease before it even hits the body. For this purpose I have arranged a semicircular cabinet on which I've placed all thirty-eight remedies (thirty-seven now Jessamy has spilled my Honeysuckle), neatly labeled, with each state of mental unhappiness clearly printed alongside. The semicircle embraces my armchair so I can easily reach any one remedy during a crisis with scarcely the movement of a full arm. Moreover, I've arranged them according to the likelihood of dilemmas occurring in my case, so that toward the central position are those remedies I've already needed, the rest descending right and left toward unlikelihood. Dead center I have placed the most vital of all, Rock Rose, the "rescue remedy," reserved for "cases where there even appears no hope."

Jessamy doesn't understand any of this. She senses only that Dr. Bach has engaged battle with her Mitsubishi because she doesn't get the usual responses to her provocations, which she has come to expect over the years. I don't pull her hair, nor storm out of the room slamming doors, nor even sulk. For in those moments when she wants me to listen to her nonsenses, I'm absorbed instead in choosing the exact flower liquid to help me combat them. This confuses and irritates her, and she begins to show signs of weakness, the tapes spinning out new and unimagined pauses in her scheme.

"I've come to stay the night."

Yes, she said that some time ago. I had taken some Crab Apple for "those who feel as if they had something not quite clean about themselves."

"Why don't you go to a hotel?"

I don't quite know what I mean by this, but it is strong enough to have brought the tapes to a halt. Jessamy has her index finger on the "hold" button. She is giving me a chance to retract for posterity, preferring to edit out such offense. I don't really care if she rewinds back to the moment we met and obliterates every millimeter of tape which follows.

No, I don't mean that. Now she's pushing me into regret. She's playing an extreme card, using memory as a weapon, and I'm beginning to resent memory itself. She is so used to deciding our mutual fate, to forecasting the future in her own favor, to stage-managing dreams and even hallucinations, that she can't abide this loss of her magical powers over me. To insure my invulnerability I'm taking a bit of White Chestnut for "those who cannot prevent thoughts, ideas, arguments which they do not desire from entering their minds."

"You'll poison yourself."

Clever. She has released the "hold" button before saying this, so the machine is again recording. My response, therefore, must be an especially careful one.

"The inside of my body has nothing to do with your autobiography."

Will this do the trick? Will it make her see, once and for all time, that we can't go on like this, moving in the rhythm of her excessive moods, without question, without proper healing?

No. Jessamy has decided the outcome of our story well in advance. Those volumes dealing with her family life, long since written out of her system ("adolescent vitriol and spittle," said a Sunday critic), will perhaps prove more kind, in the end, than those she is devoting to me. Her hatred for that rich and empty upbringing had in its grim pages at least a shred of humanity. Even the sections on her husband—whom she curiously dismisses in half a chapter ("Then I got married on paper for a few laughs and divorced two years later to bring the business full giggle")—are more charitable. I know this for a fact because she has asked me to correct the proofs of my own part, and I have been lost in the banality of her spelling while my life is being scandalized.

It was during one such proofreading session that I was introduced to the idea of "retrospective infidelity." Now I could understand such a thing in the steam of passion. But leave it to Jessamy to create ideology out of it, as she did when I told her about my first, third, and fourth wives (the second I don't dare mention, even now when it hardly matters). Anyone else, even someone far more certifiably insane than she, would have felt a pang or two, then quickly realized this was all in the far past, long before current relations were even in question, much less in progress. But Jessamy was in a screaming rage for twelve hours, then in a funk for a week, accusing me of every conceivable kind of betrayal, suggesting that, by having lovers before meeting her I was, in effect, cheating on her retrospectively.

Now even this could be swallowed, but she began to assign certain roles in her autobiography to my exwives, none of whom she had ever met. At first they were depicted more or less as harpies or witches whose spells were to blame for all the troubles between her and me. But as the chapters threatened forward into a volume she grew to like these women who had by now gained mythological proportions, which none of the scrubbers (save the second, oh the second!) deserved. They became, inevitably, sisters in a lifelong combat against myself who remained, nonetheless, completely responsible for any terrible feelings left over from her own frantic jealousy.

And so it draws itself out. Even now, despite my warnings, she is pitching her tent in readiness for some climactic tournament I am loath to fight. This is why she brings such powerful allies as Gilberto and Anita to act as her seconds and her spiritual advisers, imagining, quite falsely, that the past implies future.

I would like to pitch her headlong down flights of stairs, but my basement existence seriously limits the potential of this passion. Jessamy has removed all her clothes and stands before me expectantly.

"Are we going to bed?"

This "we," as always, implies her royal will and desire, which I'm meant to blindly follow.

"Whatever I say, you'll do just as you like."

"Yes, I will," she says.

"Then why ask?"

"I want to know if you're coming to bed with me?"

"Under no circumstances I could dream of or even nightmare of."

"I'll wait."

This last self-certainty comes from knowing me in the days before Dr. Bach. She thinks she only has to wait in the bed for some inevitable moment when I'll surely falter and rush in to her. But this time I will remain in my armchair, in the embrace of my remedies which provide a boon to my indifference.

I need a nightcap. Here's essence of Oak "for those who are struggling and fighting strongly to get well, or in connection with the affairs of their daily life. They will go on trying one thing after another, though their case may seem hopeless."

I'd really like to mix this disgusting stuff with beer, a nice long lager, it seems months. There is a can in the fridge, but the kitchen adjoins the bedroom, and I won't give her the satisfaction of thinking I'm on the way to her. Instead, I'll swallow the whole bottle of Oak, curl up in my sleeping bag here on the armchair, and recall some of the great moments of beer I've lived.

Normally Jessamy keeps the Mitsubishi running all night long so she can record any brilliances gurgled in dream-states. This is how I know that tonight, late as it has become, she is not asleep. She is not recording, but rather playing a tape, *the* tape, from *that* time, at a probable 9½ out of 10 on the volume control, of a summer night on our French island, watching our family of traveling circus Gypsies, Variétés Toulousiennes. This, of course, is a very dirty trick. She knows I do not want to be reminded of the good times, especially as I'd like to get some sleep, and yet I had better figure out why she's doing it, for this is surely just the opening gambit in what I'm beginning to sense is an all-out guerrilla attack.

We are sitting there in a tiny arena in the middle of the island, only a handful of people have come to see the performance, and this makes the players focus their efforts in our direction. Besides— as I hear Jessamy now declaring on the tape—we are radiating such powerful love energy that no one within a ten-yard radius can fail to be attracted by us. This is late evening, but we are creating immense heat in the place. For days people coming into contact with us have fainted or gone into sudden shock from energy contamination, and we are becoming known all over the island as Tristan et Isolde. In the presence of our circus artistes we seem to reach a pitch of delirium, and this makes them perform tricks which were probably unthinkable to them before that night. Long, tall, gaunt, hook-nosed, pock-marked, satin-trousered Gilberto le Jongleur is not merely tossing objects into the sky with breathless ferocity and catching them again in his six hands, but he is also climbing through hoops narrower than the girth of his body, pressing his lean frame through tight circles of cast steel. Now Anita is kicking huge circus cylinders up to heaven with her toes and at last pushing her entire body through one of these narrow cylinders while standing upright, one leg first, followed by head and arm into the abyss and—the rest of her crawling behind like a snake—pulls herself out the other side.

"At that moment," says Jessamy, now standing naked above my armchair, "we were in heat."

"It was sunstroke."

"Radioactivity!"

Shrug. I'm for cure.

"I want that heat again."

"You can't just make it happen."

"I can do anything I want!"

She wants.

"Any minute now you'll be on fire and come crawling out of your sleeping bag!"

In fact, the room is blazing hot even though there are no coins in the electric meter. But I remain well zipped. She thinks, as always, that by heating each other up, in one rush of collective sweat in a mutual bed, that we are somehow magically healed. She doesn't understand, you see, that I simply can't forget the hurts she has done me, the venom heaped on me when she says I haven't loved her enough or when she suspects me of infidelities I'm not about to commit, not to mention my broken jawbone when she battered me with her microphone.

Now she's trying to force her way into my sleeping bag, but I'm holding the zipper fast from the inside. She threatens to cut the bag open with a razor, and I know she will do it without stopping to consider the depth of her cut. She is so caught up in the idea that she is neglecting to record it. Gilberto and Co. continue to perform on the tape. To divert her attention, I point out her oversight, and she is momentarily perplexed. Should she carry on her assault without history listening, or does she dare back off from me—risking my possible escape—to try again when it can form a blustering climax to her story? Quickly she chooses a third option—which I have not considered in my getaway plans—pulling me by the hair so that I am dragged along with her on the floor until she can reach the tape recorder. Now she sits on my head to hold me fast while she puts on a fresh tape. There is no hope for me unless I can, by some miracle, turn myself toward the bottom of the bag, which has another zipper moving in the opposite direction. I'm trying to open it with my toes, but this is out of the question. Jessamy has switched on the new tape to record the scene, and drags me now toward the bathroom to find a razor. As she turns away I slip my head beneath the canvas and, in homage to Anita and her contortions, draw my legs up to my chest. The bag is far too narrow for a full turn, but Jessamy is unknowingly helping me by pulling at the top of it, providing force for me to struggle against while moving toward the bottom. Just as we reach the cold bathroom floor my hair catches in the top zipper, and I rip some of it trying to free myself. She must have noticed this because she is kicking me viciously from outside the bag. She sees what I'm up to, but I must hope she doesn't know about the bottom zipper. I hear her begin to cut fiercely through the bag, knowing she will go right through my skin. With one last prayer to St. Anita of the Cylinder I manage to force my legs over my head, and the quick approach of the razor permits the impossible to occur in a desperate moment. Now facing the bottom of the bag I force the zipper quickly round to get out just as Jessamy jumps at me razor first. She has cut my finger and keeps slashing at me, but a swift kick in the chest puts her out of action. It won't be for long. Running to the kitchen I find a meat cleaver handy for self-defense, but it is useless since Jessamy is much faster than me. I need a weapon that can hold her at some distance, outside slashing range. On the floor is a mop in a bucket of filthy water. My timing is perfect: she raises her hand to cut me and gets the bilge mop smack in her mouth.

Some hours later I begin to worry about Jessamy's crushing defeat. It has always been essential for her to win, but now she seems to lie in the bed in disgrace, making fearful sobbing noises and shifting the mattress violently. I have never known her to take it this way, without further assault, without some unexpected conjuring trick. Perhaps she is still plotting her revenge. And yet I have been able to sleep for some hours, peacefully in my armchair, despite the shredded sleeping bag, waking only when I heard her soft crying. I could not have rested if there were fresh battle to come.

The most curious of Dr. Bach's chapters is one called "Over-Care for Welfare of Others." I think I need one of these remedies to halt my mounting sympathy. Vine is for "very capable people, certain of their own ability, confident of success. Being so assured, they think that it would be for the benefit of others if they could be persuaded to do things as they themselves do, or as they are certain is right." That's actually for Jessamy, not for me, but I'll swallow it anyway on her behalf.

Her shrieking intensifies. I can see, over there at the foot of the bedroom door (now slightly ajar) that she has put on a new tape to catch her dreams, leaving the machine nonetheless in a place where she can record my actions too. Staring at the ever-turning spools I suddenly wonder how she has had the presence of mind—in somber defeat—to make this new preparation. Something also tells me she is going too far with her sobbing, which is no longer sobbing, but something else quite familiar, designed to confuse me and put me off guard. I know this special wailing of hers—although it is some months since I myself provoked it—but I can't see what she hopes to gain by simulating it on her own. Perhaps she is trying to plant these sounds in her tape recorder so that, years from now, she can convince herself (and her public) that I really did come to her bed this night. I wouldn't put it past her. Nonetheless, she is carrying it to extremes, talking out loud as if I were actually in the room with her, bouncing fitfully on the mattress for a bit of tape verité. It even increases in velocity, and the bed begins to bang up against the wall, shaking the entire flat with her lunacies. In this, to her everlasting damnation, she overturns some of my remedies, including the irreplaceable Rock Rose, "the remedy of emergency for cases where there even appears no hope." Quickly I salvage some, still rocking precariously on the cabinet, but at my feet is a mess of broken bottles and running liquid.

I must quickly shout down this madwoman before she destroys everything. But now I notice, for the first time, that the front window is open. I certainly didn't open it, and it was closed before I fell asleep. I will ask her about it. Yet something stops me at the door of the bedroom. There are two voices inside, barking at each other in syncopation of passions. I try the front door. Locked and bolted. I listen again at the bedroom. Knowing Jessamy, she would have learned ventriloquism just to play this trick on me. And yet there are shafts of heat coming through the door, as only she can create in combination. But if I push the door open and fall into her trap, she will greet me with a victorious grin to prove she has unsettled me. Instead I'll close the window and go back to sleep, letting her continue her solo performance without an audience. Clearly she has opened the window to make me worry that someone has got in, despite the iron bars which cover it. . . . So.

So. . . . So Jessamy is bucking heavenward in spasms, gurgling in French, accompanied by the clear, undeniable sound of a male voice. So I, my limbs wracked by illness and distress, cannot perform such miracles of muscular abandon. So she gains her freedom by bringing these hot memories somehow to fleshy life in my bedroom, spilling my flower remedies, laughing at me all the way to this crescendo of shrieks. So I'll wait till they subside so she can hear me kicking in her Mitsubishi.

A week later a letter arrives from Jessamy, posted the day after I threw her out into the street. Jessamy lives half a mile from here. Why has this letter taken a week to arrive? In 1912, Kafka, writing to his girlfriend would post his letters at six in the evening in Prague, so she'd be sure to get them the following morning in Berlin. In this way, he could be sure that he still stood by whatever he had written at the moment she was reading it. Such clarity is denied to us in these times, in these places where a letter takes seven days to travel half a mile.

So I'm led to wonder: what does Jessamy believe now, or even, where can Jessamy be while I am reading:

To Whom It May Concern,
Enclosed please find my bill (estimate) of £17.50 for repair of one Mitsubishi tape recorder. As I am without the services of this machine for some weeks, I am compelled to "hold," and have decided to use the time to revise those passages in my autobiography which refer to you. Here is the first paragraph for you to proofread:
"X creates his own diseases. Most often he is not aware of his reasons for bringing about a particular disease. Sometimes, he believes so strongly in his diseases that he takes them for granted, like lifelong friends. What he doesn't realize is that by trying to heal his diseases he is transforming his own physical reality. The energy released in this transformation does not die. It goes somewhere, and where it goes depends on what X believes and wants. If he manages to heal an ailment, his mind sends it to another place, perhaps one which allows it to grow more dangerously. In this way, X guides his life through a series of diseases, which he refuses to accept as guideposts to an understanding of himself. His attempts at so-called "healing" are nothing but self-deception, and display a lack of trust for his own spontaneous being and nature.
X is, at the moment, an addict of Dr. Bach's remedies,

which are nothing more than harmless herbs mixed with distilled water. He wastes countless hours swallowing these, when his real "cure" lies perhaps in hot places which have street energy, night energy, heat energy, and languages which are not his own. In such places, and only in such places, can X realize that we do not need to be healed, only to live our dying to the full."

Please do send me the corrected text by return of post.

Yours Faithfully,

Etc.

I must answer this arrogance, even if it means venturing outside to post a letter. She has really stirred it up now, and I must even scrap my determination never to contact her again. She has me all wrong, judging me as usual by criteria she uses on herself. If nothing else, she must be told how hopelessly out of date she is. The Bach remedies, failing to cure me of her, lie accordingly at the bottom of my rubbish bin. I am, however, reading up on aroma therapy and have discovered that my true cure, given my birthdate, my sensibility, my personal nature, is a rubdown solution derived from essence of marigolds which I have sent for a week ago, and which would long since have arrived were this another town, another time.

TWO POEMS

WILLIAM HEINESEN

Translated from the Danish by Hedin Brønner

TRANSLATOR'S NOTE. *The Nobel Prize in Literature for 1981 would certainly have gone to the Faroe Islander, William Heinesen, had he not heard of his own candidacy and renounced the impending honor. He dismayed his friends, of course, but they respected the motives he gave for this unusual act. He had felt that the award should not go to a Faroese author who has been writing in Danish rather than in his own native language, which is a rare and archaistic relative of Norwegian.*

But there was no need for such diffidence on his part. For all his use of Danish in his writing—a natural thing for most educated people in the Faroes of his youth—William Heinesen is a fire-breathing patriot, as inseparable from his own soil as the crazily tilted sheeplands there, or the dizzy fowling cliffs, or the capricious tides and currents that swirl around the rocky shoreline.

And in any case, the domination of the Danish language over the Faroese for hundreds of years was due to an accident of history that had nothing to do with the Nobel Prize or with William Heinesen, as explained in the notes to those uninhibited prose fantasies of his, "The Flies" and "The Gryla," in ND38 and ND40.

To offer a glimpse of William Heinesen's wizardry in leaping from one art form to another, we are presenting two poems from his collection Panorama med Regnbue (Panorama with Rainbow), *published by Gyldendal, Copenhagen, in 1972. They show qualities usually associated with much younger artists: a mood of protest and a penchant for the original and the experimental.*

Born in 1900, William Heinesen is still going strong, devoting most of his time to graphic art and the short story. His international reputation is based largely on his spirited and whimsical fiction, but it was as a poet and painter that he was first recognized in his own homeland over fifty years ago.—H.B.

ARCTIS

The warming scent
of slumbering men and beasts
under the roofs of huts and houses
hangs yet in his clothing
and in his ear yet dwells
a resonance of warm voices,
an echo of the sound
of unforgettable dear names.
But before him unfold the silent night
and the wastes of the nameless lands.

As the plucked flower
longs back to its root in the soil
so longs he back
to the land of living voices,
to the pleasant warmth that streams
from the laughter and tears and mild eyes
of days submerged forever.
Before him lies a land
without words and names—
a far-stretched land
whose center knows no compass points:
the farthest land
where the journey ends.

A GREAT FLOCKING ROUND THE ANCHORITE

It is night it is morning not
morning it is midday antimidday
over the desert or rather actually
paris where crowds of us are on our
way to the sacred st samuels cave why
just see our marvelous cara
van we are world reporters out
standing euroasiamerican newsmen with
corporations backing us megaphonists radiomacro
logists of progress and destruc
tion tv tyrannosaurs in
short all the blessings of the presentday cul
tural front lines with the worlds best liter
ary beans in our avantgarde unfortun
ately we never saw moses smash the tablets never
empedocles plunge into etnas crater never
you socrates drain your last shocktail never
you pilate wash your hands god in heaven
what front page material for millions never
peter the apostle chop van goghs ear off never
and now that einstein freud and all the great
of our time are gone proust joyce tho
mas mann eliot etc now there is no real sup
erstar except beckett who has lived here in
the loneliness of the desert for many years and liv
ed on thorns and thistles they say hes still alive we
ll soon be there the avantgardists are there already
with their existential jimmy that opens every
lock now we are waiting for godot oh look now theyre
dragging our terrible alienated lazarus out
of the cabinet is he furious no only abashed his
distinctive mummy face with its faded irish
eyes who has bravely set all the values of life
down to way below the treeline this
anchorite of negations who taught
us disgust at life as well as death there he
stands tortured in the flash of all sorts of

eager publicity hear his tired voice
nomming? non rien n'est nommable
dire? non rien n'est dicible
so now thats been said hasnt it announces
the avantgarde enthusiastically that was the quint
essence what our western culture fin
ally has reached through thousands of years of som
ersaults and now just one last snap
shot so no he wont take off his
breeches for the tabloids no yes by god now
they all sing for he is a jolly good fellow strong
tushing from the ivory tower but
after all we are good fellows and so we let
him go in peace our immortal little one just
go in and lie down in the box again
dear old worrywart and concentrate
yet once again quite hydrogenbomblewdly on
NOTHING
for thats one thing we children of the affluent societies
never can get enough of.

FOUR POEMS

TERRY KISTLER

CAGE SIGHT

Silent from within a roped lacing of cage
a white bird seamed with blue slow sees
the door open near and cats dropping to walk
toe to toe from stone stairs to iron

garden gate and fox eyes shining in the dark
dew-flecked web of field as large-taloned
hunting birds lift and turn in a sky white

and far as a door itself beyond where he
began to remember in the valley of its blue
his own striped ancestors wings reaching.

NATURALIST AMONG SUMMER FLORA

The grapes and spotted peaches are woven
into the white bowl and silent heat
and in these hours as crowded as the lake shore
with tables of rock lichen and blooming flora

the broad descent of the sun takes its end out
among the crossing hills and valley mountains.

And rising from thick microscope lenses
I gather myself toward the shaded veins
and column of her sleep, her hand single
upon a book, her head separate in hair.

And stirring she lets breathe her wakened length,
saying, I've missed your long arms dark in mine.
And now I lift the rumpled silk back
from beside her throat, edge back and let
the focus of my eyes surround her shoulder
in a force I have not felt within these

diagrams of order. O now what clouded
lights of form move as instinct and lift
to release their hidden harmony as each
shift of hand leads in and links unhinged

to her soft transmitted images of sense,
the fuel of the blood preparing each touch
and each thought of touch and each memory
as it was, a different life lived but short
in another time and remembered exact
within this slow surrender of arm and shoulder.

O now once more let the wind of passion
fall over us as the storms of afternoon
through these lake pine standing strong
within the curving limbs of one another.

WOMAN MASK

I spread down again, distant, flat, dim,
faultless as sand wrapping around him.

It is different yet the same.
I have not known how they can make

so much of it. Is it not that way
for them, the new differences
edged around? Blue eyes. Brown eyes.
Long fingers. So little to choose.

Incidentals in such a sameness.
There are the old and the burnt-over
lovers of course. There is a certain
elegance, an ease in them. And the painters,

their careless force. Yet at an end
they come to the same. And I have my clothes,
bright, rich and separate pieces.
My fish still more complete. My birds.

I feed them and they swim or sing.
I bury them. When they die I wrap them
and drive into the country and bury them.
It too is the same always, their flesh

stiff to the soft, shoveled earth. Yet
I never tire of their need and their
simplicity. Effortless travelers,
effortlessly going with me.

AH VISITORS

The door cannot disagree
with the space it leaves
as it opens into the room

nor can the writer regain

the words that move his hand
as they enter into the fixed insignia

and not even the sitter resist
the changeless face that draws his force
as he turns toward memory,

the vines, however, go on
extending their separate tendrils
too close to the garden trellis
to wake the hidden shade.

Ah vistors, ah universal wilderness
of act, I saw the lamp swing
when you led this present
so far into my life.

A BOND FOR TWO LIFETIMES—
GLEANINGS

FUMIKO ENCHI

Translated from the Japanese by Phyllis Birnbaum

Kneeling down on my knees in the veranda, I called out through the faded, patched sliding door,

"Professor, is it all right if I come in?"

From within came his unclear, thick reply which could have been yes or no, and there was the muffled sound of his bedclothes as he shifted position in bed. Since I knew this was his usual answer, I softly slid open the door and, still in my overcoat, I went in.

As I had anticipated, Professor Nunokawa had lifted his head, with its rumpled white hair, up from the rather dirty pillow and was just then groping for the large, thin revised edition of his book that lay at the side of the pallet. Every time I came to take notes for him, I noticed the dirty fuzziness of the coarse sheets and the strip of white fabric attached to the edge of the quilt. The maid, Mineko, who looked after the professor, seemed to let many days go by without changing the linen. Even a young person in a fetid sickbed would look quite miserable; an old man lying in such a state seemed even more appalling.

I didn't know when my feelings of pity or compassion had actually turned into an abhorrence of this wretchedness. Even as my abhorrence grew with each breath I took of the steamy mildewed smell of the sickroom, I inquired soothingly after the professor's health. Before she had gone out to shop, Mineko had evidently made preparations for my visit by drawing an old sandalwood desk, whose sheen had utterly vanished, close to the side of the bed. I spread my notebook out on the top of it.

The professor had a hot-water bottle in his bed. Since the few pieces of charcoal in the small china brazier were forever going out, the room became bitingly cold on days like today when the early winter rains occasionally mixed with snow. Following the suggestion the professor had made at our first session, I kept my coat on and sat through each meeting still dressed for the outdoors.

"Today we're going to do 'A Bond for Two Lifetimes,' aren't we?"

The professor didn't want to discuss his illness, and so he lay face up and opened the thin book on his chest. He took a red pencil in his right hand and looked at me by moving only his eyes behind his thick-rimmed spectacles. On the desk, I opened the same revised version of *Tales of Spring Rain* that the professor held.

"Page fifty-nine is where 'A Bond for Two Lifetimes' begins," I said.

The professor was working on colloquial versions of Ueda Akinari's *Tales of Moonlight and Rain* and *Tales of Spring Rain*, which would become a volume in a series of Edo literary works put out by the publishing company I worked for. I had undertaken to act as secretary for Professor Nunokawa, my former teacher, as he dictated, since he was apparently unable to write for himself. Even though he was sick, he had worked up much enthusiasm for this colloquial translation because he needed the money.

I had already finished recording the colloquial version of the nine gothic tales from *Tales of Moonlight and Rain* and had completed the first five stories in *Tales of Spring Rain*, all dictated by the professor through lips, puckered in their toothlessness, which narrated the stories carefully and almost without hesitation like a silkworm spitting out thread. In *Tales of Spring Rain*, a work of Akinari's later years, the preface states:

"How many days has it been now that the rains of spring have brought this touching quiet? I picked up my usual writing brush and inkstone and thought over various matters but found I had nothing to write. Copying the old-fashioned storytelling styles is a job for the amateur writer, but I, living like a mountain rustic, have hardly any subjects to write about. I have been deceived into believing in the things people have described about the past and the present, and, thinking them true, have related these tales to others, thus deceiving them as well. In any case, there will be people who, as the tales are told, will continue to take these made-up stories as real situations. Yet I'll continue to tell tales while the rains of spring fall."

With these words in mind, the old author seemed to feel he had progressed beyond *Tales of Moonlight and Rain*, which had delicately spun novelistic details together, and now dismissed his old style of writing as "a job for the amateur writer." Nevertheless, he continued to record his dark, hidden, and uncontrollable passions freely, boldly, and without constraint, these being dramatized by historical personages, in folklore, and legends. There are many stories in *Tales of Spring Rain* which diverge from accepted feudal morality, so it was to be expected that the work did not become as popular as *Tales of Moonlight and Rain*, and not many copies were handed down through the generations.

In his later years, Akinari's old wife had died. He also had no children and the sight in his left eye had gone. For a considerable period of time, he lived in a faintly illumined world, troubled by problems of food and clothing and shelter. Professor Nunokawa had established a reputation as a scholar of Edo literature. His oldest son had died during the war and his wife had also passed away. His only daughter, who was married, hardly ever came to see him because of his uncompromising character and also because she hated the fact that Mineko was always around.

Without either pension or annuity, the professor could continue the revision of manuscripts and dictation only because he had the help of a mere two or three of his students in his old age. While he was translating *Tales of Moonlight and Rain*, I had not noticed as much, but by the time we got to *Tales of Spring Rain*, I was often struck by the similarity of Akinari's last years and the present life of Professor Nunokawa. There were times when the professor's dictation sounded as if it emanated quite spontaneously from an essential source within his own core. The professor stood the book on his chest and he began to speak gently in the low voice people use to commence recitations of Buddhist prayers.

"During one autumn in Yamashiro province, all the leaves had fallen from the tall zelkova trees. The strong chilly wind blew down over a mountain village. It was cold and exceedingly lonely. There was a rich landowner whose family had lived in Kosobe village for many years. They owned many mountain fields and lived in such comfort that the family did not worry nor make a commotion if the harvests were good or bad.

"Thus the head of the house quite naturally read books as his hobby and made no effort to seek friends among the village people. Every day, until late at night, he read books under his lamp. His mother would worry about this.

" 'Shouldn't you be going to bed soon? The temple bell has already struck twelve. Father always used to say that if you stay up late at night reading books, you will wear yourself out and end up ill. When people enjoy doing something, they tend to immerse themselves completely in their own entertainments without being aware of what is happening. Then they regret it later,' she said, offering him her views on the subject.

"He took her warning as a sign of motherly affection for him and, feeling grateful to her, resolved to be in bed after the clock struck ten. One night the rain fell gently, and in the stillness that had settled from early evening no other sound was heard. Consequently, he got so lost in his reading that much time passed without him realizing it. This night he forgot his mother's warning, and when he opened the window, thinking that it might be two o'clock in the morning, the rain had stopped, there was no wind and the late-night moon had risen in the middle sky.

" 'Ah, what a quiet night it is! I should write a poem about this moment,' he said, and, rubbing an inkstick over the inkslab, took up his writing brush. He put his mind to one or two poetic lines, and while inclining his head and trying to think of more, he happened to hear something like a bell ringing among the chirping of the insects, until then the only sounds. Strange, he said to himself, now that he thought about it, this was not the first time that he had heard the sound of this bell. He absorbed for the first time the odd realization that every night when he had been reading his books like this, he had heard that same noise. When he got up and went into the garden to have a look here and there to find the source of the sound of the bell, he went to the place he thought the noise had originated, beneath a stone in the corner of the garden where there was a clump of unmowed grasses. After making sure that this was where the sound was coming from, he returned to his bedroom.

"The next day he called his servants together and ordered them to dig beneath the stone. When they had dug down three feet, their shovels struck a large rock. After removing that rock, they saw something which resembled a coffin with a lid on it. Expending great effort, they lifted off the heavy lid, and when they looked inside, they found a peculiar object which now and then rang a bell it held in its hand.

"When the head of the house, followed by the servants, came close and nervously had a look, they saw a form which might have been a human being, and then again might not. Its appearance was parched and hard, shrivelled up like a dried-up salmon, and bony. The hair had grown long and hung down to the knees. The head of the house ordered a strong servant to pick the thing up and carefully bring it out of the coffin. The man exclaimed when he had picked up the body.

'It's light, very light, like nothing at all. Doesn't seem to have an old man's ripe smell,' he said loudly, half frightened.

"Even when the people lifted the thing out, the hand kept on ringing the bell. The head of the house looked upon the object, and he reverently clasped his hands together and prayed, saying to the others: 'This is what is called "entering a trance," which is one of the ways priests die, as Buddhism teaches. While still alive, some priests sit down in their caskets and die while meditating. This is what must have happened to this person. Our family has been living in this place for over one hundred years, and since I have never heard anything about such an event, it must have occurred before our ancestors came here. Did his soul go to paradise and only his undecayed flesh remain here? And what tenacity, to have only his hand keep ringing the bell as before. Since we have dug him up, let's see if we can bring him back to life.'

"The head of the house helped the servants bring this thing, dried and hard like a wooden statue, into the house.

" 'Be careful! Don't bump against the post and smash it,' he said, as though they were carrying a breakable item. Finally it was placed in one of the rooms, and carefully covered with quilts. The head of the house filled a teacup with lukewarm water, came to the thing's side and pressed the liquid upon the dried lips. Then, a black object like a tongue emerged sluggishly and licked its lips and soon seemed to be sucking eagerly at the cotton wad soaked in water. Upon seeing this, the women and children raised their voices in terror, 'How horrifying, horrifying! It's a ghost!' and ran out, refusing to come near again. The head of the house, encouraged by the changes in the thing, treated the dried-up creature with care. His mother joined him in giving it lukewarm water, each time remembering to utter a Buddhist prayer. During the passage of about fifty days, the face, hands, and legs, which had been like dried salmon, regained their moisture bit by bit, and some body warmth seemed to have been restored.

" 'Truly, he's coming back to life!' the head of the house said and doubled his care and ministrations. As a result, the eyes opened for the first time. He moved his eyes toward the light but didn't seem to see clearly. When he was fed rice water and weak porridge, he moved his tongue and seemed to taste. He seemed to behave like an ordinary person whom you might find anywhere. The wrinkles on his skin, previously like the bark of an old tree, stretched out and he put on more flesh. He could move his arms and legs more freely. He seemed to be able to hear, for when he became aware of the gusts of the north wind, his naked body shivered as though he were chilled. When he was offered some old padded clothes, he put out his hands to receive the offering with great pleasure. He also developed an appetite.

"At the beginning, when the head of the house had thought of the man as the reincarnation of a revered personage, he had treated him with respect and did not dream of giving him the unholy flesh of fish to eat. When the new arrival, however, saw the others partaking of fish, he licked his lips to indicate how much he hungered for it. And when such foods were put upon his tray the guest gnawed at the bones and ate every single bit with great gusto. The head of the house felt his spirits sink.

"Then the master asked him politely, 'You have gone into a trance once and it has been your unusual fate to return from the dead. To make this religious experience more inspiring to us, could you tell us about what it was like living for such a long time beneath the earth?'

"The man just shook his head and said, 'I know nothing,' and looked stupidly into the master's face.

" 'Even so, can you not at least remember what happened when you went into the ground? In your previous life, what name did they call you?'

"The man was thus questioned, but could recall nothing. He became bashful, moved back, sucked his finger and was no different from any doltish peasant farmer from the area.

All his efforts of the past several months, and his exaltation in the belief that he had restored some worthy cleric to life having come to nothing, the master was thoroughly disheartened by the turn of events. Afterwards, he treated the man like a servant and had him sweep the garden and sprinkle the water. Not seeming to mind in the least such menial work, he was not lazy as he went about his chores.

" 'Buddha's teachings are quite ridiculous. Where has all that piety gone which was supposed to be strong enough to put him in a trance, and to sustain him there for over one hundred years buried in the earth, and to cause him to tap his handbell? There's no trace of nobility in his character. What is it supposed to mean that only his body has come back to life?' the master of the house said and others in the village also joined him, knitting their brows in consternation."

"Let's stop there for now."

The professor had turned to rest on his side without my noticing it. He listlessly put down the book which he had been holding until then.

"You must be tired. Shall I bring you tea?"

"No," he said, pursing his lips sourly. "Has Mine come back? I must go to the bathroom. Could you call her for me?"

I got up very quickly and slid open the room divider. I called out in a high-pitched voice to Mineko, already back from her shopping and apparently somewhere in the kitchen.

"Mineko! Mineko! The professor has to urinate!"

The professor had problems with his bladder and urinated with difficulty. He usually used a catheter to relieve himself, but since there had been one time during his dictation when he had felt sudden discomfort and had ended by soiling himself, I became a bit frenzied.

The rumor was that the professor had nicknamed Mineko "Goddess of the Narrow Eyes," * and when she—with her slits for eyes and flabby white flesh—came running in from the kitchen, I switched places with her and went into the adjoining family room. There Mineko seemed to have been working on her knitting, for the red sweater she was in the process of making lay on top of the dirty printed cotton brazier cover and had two or three knitting needles stuck in it. Since the room was cold, I surreptitiously slipped my hands under the brazier cover and, listening to what was taking place in the next room, guessed that Mineko had slid the urinal under the professor.

"There! Now a little more . . . Lift yourself up a bit more, that's it, now we're fine," she said, raising her voice as if issuing commands, and then she said bluntly, between gasps, "Professor, it's time you dismissed Mrs. Noritake, isn't it . . . Well isn't it . . . It's time you dismissed . . ."

"No. Not yet. We're just taking a break. You finish this up now."

"Take your time. I'm just organizing my notes," I called in.

The professor did not answer. The insertion of the narrow rubber tube must have been painful.

"Oh, that hurts. Don't be so rough!" His carping voice came to my ears a number of times like moans, and no sooner did I realize that he had stopped scolding than I heard the thin trickle of urine splashing into the urinal through the tubing—a sound that expressed only too bleakly the meager store of the professor's life.

More than ten years had passed since I had graduated from my women's college. Professor Nunokawa, who was a teacher there, favored me a great deal by lending me books and having me help him with his research. During that time, with a boldness that astonished me, he would rub his body against mine, squeeze my hand and brazenly make advances suggesting further intimacies. Since I was engaged to my husband at the time—he was later killed in the war—and was just about to get married, I took the professor's advances as a middle-aged man's impudence. I found him altogether repugnant and sustained my contempt throughout our relationship.

I looked back on these incidents in the light of the scandals that had brewed in those days over the professor's lechery, which were

* Goddess who, according to ancient myth, performed a rousing dance, baring her body, to tempt the Sun Goddess from the cave where she had hidden and left the world in darkness.

so thoroughly unbecoming a teacher. I now realized that the energies of a man in the prime of his life must have been brimming over his body. The professor had nicknamed me Tamakazura, after the daughter of Prince Genji's great love, and at about that time, I myself lost my husband, barely a year after my marriage. He had been a technical officer in the navy and was killed in an air raid upon a military base in the homeland. I was a bereft war widow with a young boy to look after, living a marginal existence in the ten years since the end of the war.

As a woman alone, and working in those harsh postwar conditions, I encountered many bald advances from various men, of a sort even worse than Professor Nunokawa's. But I came to typify the proverb "A woman widowed in her twenties will be able to live forever without remarrying," because I felt both my mind and body fully, naturally moistened and blossoming from the mere year or more of contact with my husband. Whether for good or ill, I had passed these months and years without the opportunity of becoming attached to a second man. Now past thirty and holding down a job in a publishing house, I might appear to others to be a woman as parched in body and soul as the dried-up salmon in the story. But deep within my being, I sometimes embrace my husband in my dreams and I often feel the miracle of seeing my husband's visage quite vividly in the face of my small son.

As a result, I have recently begun to view the inevitable sexual aggressions of men with a sympathetic eye. When I realized that for the unprincipled Professor Nunokawa, who had in the past paid court to me tenaciously, life meant the putting of all his energies into producing a paltry quantity of urine in the next room, my whole being shook and I was brought very close to tears.

When I was called in again and entered the room, Mineko, disposing of the urinal, had vanished behind the sliding doors. It may have been my imagination, but the professor seemed to have more color in his face as he leaned upon one elbow on the pillow.

"What do you think of this story? It's interesting, isn't it?" the professor asked me, enthusiastically.

"Very much so. I didn't know that there was such an interesting story in *Tales of Spring Rain*. Was it taken from another source?"

"Naturally," he said and the learned professor spoke to me about

"The Attachment Which Plagued the Trance," a story from *The Old Woman's Teatime Stories,* on which Akinari had apparently based his story. In 1653, a priest named Keitatsu of the Seikan Temple on Mt. Myotsu in Yamato-Kōriyama was about to go into his trance. Suddenly, he became infatuated with a beautiful woman visiting the temple and was unable to attain enlightenment. Fifty-five years later, still unable to subdue his own soul, he was beating his handbell and drum.

"The preface to *The Old Woman's Teatime Stories* dates from the early 1740's, probably written when Akinari was a child. In any case, since the work comes from that period, he wouldn't have been able to get a copy easily and so Akinari might have read it decades later. If Akinari had written this story in the same frame of mind as when he had written *Tales of Moonlight and Rain,* I think he might have described the part about the priest's infatuation with the beautiful woman in more detail."

As I listened to him say this, I lowered my eyes and thought that the professor might be expressing something of his own feelings here.

"Actually there's another story told about this. *A History of Fictional Biographies,* written by Tsubouchi Shoyo and Mizutani Futo in the Meiji period, relates the story of Aeba Koson, who had heard about a man who had supposedly seen the manuscript version of Akinari's *A Tale of Rainy Nights.* According to the story, *A Tale of Rainy Nights* resembled this "A Bond for Two Lifetimes," but the ending is quite different. They are similar up to the point where the bell sounds below the ground, but then the story goes on to say that the man who hears the bell himself digs a hole. There he finds an old Buddhist priest who had gone into a trance and had been reciting sutras with fierce concentration. So the man brought the priest out above the ground, and under the light of the moon, they opened their hearts to each other and discussed many a matter. Even this format, religious questions and answers, was quite possible for Akinari."

"But this version is more typical of Akinari, don't you think, Professor?" I said, objecting.

The story of the fanatical faith of a priest who had gone into a trance and wholeheartedly recited the sutras for decades, but had still been unable to free himself from the mortal encumbrances of skin and bones might have been pleasing irony for the argumentative Akinari, since it showed how firm belief does not necessarily bring the expected rewards. But for me, the latter part of the story which the professor was now translating into colloquial Japanese had by far a more fulsome eeriness and deep pathos.

"Ha, ha, ha," the professor laughed weakly, his sharp Adam's apple twitching. "You want that to happen to you, don't you? That's perfectly natural. You would like to have a bond that extends over two lifetimes."

It was in the professor's nature, when he felt better, to utter witticisms that were not exactly in good taste.

"I still have time. If you're not tired, shall we go to the end of the story?" I said, edging up to the desk.

"Yes, let's try. If we can get through with this, we'll be able to finish the rest easily."

The professor lay down on his back again and opened the book on his chest.

"We did up to here, didn't we . . . 'Really, the teachings of Buddhism serve no benefit. He entered the earth like this and rang his bell for over one hundred years. How fruitless that there is no trace of it and only the bones remain . . .'?"

"Yes, that's where we left off."

"Upon observing the dimwittedness of this man, the mother of the head of the house gradually changed her whole attitude toward life.

" 'For these many years, I have thought only of avoiding suffering in the world hereafter. I have been extraordinarily generous in my almsgiving and charity at the temple. Morning and evening, I never fail to utter a Buddhist prayer. When I look at this man here right in front of my eyes, I feel I have been duped by a sly fox or cunning badger,' she said and even told this to her son.

"Save for visiting the tombs of her parents and husband, she abandoned her religious duties. Not caring a bit for the opinions of her neighbors, she went off on moon-viewing picnics and when the cherry blossoms bloomed, and, taking along her daughter-in-law and her grandchildren, was concerned only with enjoying herself.

" 'I visit with my relatives often and pay more attention to the servants. Occasionally I give them things. I now live in peace and ease, having completely forgotten that I felt grateful for the chance to utter Buddhist prayers and listen to sermons,' the mother would say to people. As if loosed from chafing restraints, she behaved in quite a youthful, lively manner.

"Although the disinterred man was usually quite absentminded, he would get angry if he didn't get enough to eat or if someone scolded him. At these times, he would knit his brows and mutter complaints. The servants and the local people stopped treating him with even the slightest trace of reverence, and in his name alone, Jōsuke of the Trance, remained traces of the fact that he had entered into a trance and had come back to life. For five years, he remained as a servant in this house.

"In this village there was a poor widow. This woman was also regarded as rather stupid, and at some point she became intimate with Jōsuke of the Trance. He was seen diligently cultivating her tiny fields and washing the pots and kettles in the back stream. Since only circumstances had forced him to agree to employ Jōsuke and keep him for the rest of his life, his master, once this state of affairs became known, smiled wryly and, along with everyone else, actively encouraged Jōsuke to enter into an alliance with the woman, and Jōsuke finally became the woman's husband.

"Rumors flourished:

'He says he doesn't even know how old he is, but he seems to remember quite well how men and women behave together.'

'Very true. On the face of it, there seems to be a reason for Jōsuke's return to earth. Everyone thought he had been down in that hole ringing his bell morning and evening because of a pious wish for Buddha's providence. So, he actually was set upon coming back to our floating world of pleasure only to have sex, eh? What a noble desire that was!'

"The young people of the village went to great lengths to investigate how Jōsuke and the widow were carrying on. When they peeped in through the crevices of the wooden door of the dilapidated house, it was no monster they saw cavorting with a woman. They returned home dispirited.

"'In spite of all the religious principles about cause and effect which Buddhism teaches, when we see such an example before our very eyes, all our faith vanishes.'

"This became the common talk among the people of the village. Almsgiving to the temples in Kosobe declined, and in the neighboring villages as well.

"The chief priest of the temple, whose family had enjoyed a prestigious position in the village for a long time, noticed these changed attitudes most. It is quite difficult for people living in this earthly world to fathom how Buddhist salvation, so beyond mortal imagination, is effected. But he could not condone the destruction of the belief in Buddhist virtues on account of the events taking place before his very eyes. He resolved to investigate when it was that Jōsuke had entered into his trance, and at least to resolve the terrible confusion in the minds of these foolish men and women.

"He consulted the temple's death registry and questioned every elder of the village. He made such efforts to find the buried truth about Jōsuke that he forgot to perform the required services at the temple. Unfortunately, after a big flood in the village over one hundred and fifty years ago, the houses and villagers had all been washed away. Moreover, a new branch in the river had emerged and the topography changed. After the irrigation facilities had improved, the people started living there once again.

"Thus, where the village was before the flood now corresponded to a place somewhere in the middle of the river. Since the region now called Kosobe was formerly at the sandy bank of the river where no houses had stood, it was impossible to discover why the coffin of the priest had been buried there.

" 'But if the holy saint had been trapped in the flood, water must have poured into his mouth and ears. Afterward he dried up and hardened. Then he must have been turned into the dullard that Jōsuke is today.' Some people expressed such views with utterly serious expressions, while others spoke mockingly. But the question of Jōsuke's past was no closer to a solution.

"The mother of the village headman had lived eighty long years and she became quite sick. When she was near death, she called her doctor and said,

'Now I am fully prepared to die, although until now, I have not known when my time would come. I have lived up to now because of the medicines you have given me. You have taken good care of me for many years. Please continue to take care of my family after this. My son is already sixty years old, but he is weak-willed and dependent. I worry very much about him. Please give him advice now and then and tell him not to let the family fortunes fail.'

"The son, who was the village headman, heard this and smiled bitterly,

'I am already old enough to have white hair on my head. By nature I am a bit dull-witted, but I have listened to all you have taught and will do my best for the family. Please don't worry about this world of ours, just chant your Buddhist prayers and die in peace,' he said, but the sick woman looked at the doctor in some distress, and said,

'Just listen to him, doctor. You see the fool that has been such an affliction to me. At this point in my life, I have no intention of being reborn in paradise if praying to the Buddha is the only way to do it. If, due to lack of faith, I am reborn an animal and have to suffer, I don't think that's particularly terrible. Having lived so long and observed all sorts of creatures in this world, it seems to me that even cows and horses, so often made the symbols for pain, don't actually lead a life only of suffering. In fact, they seem to enjoy happy and contented moments too. Buddhism tells us that human beings are expected to live in a world far superior to that inhabited by cows and horses, but now that I think of it, I can count on my fingers the number of pleasurable moments I've had. And how I've had less free time each day than any cow or horse! Year in, year out, we have to dye our clothes new colors and wash them. Aside from such everyday tasks, at the end of the year, if we neglect to pay tribute to our master, it means punishment, for us a calamity of the first order . . . And just when we are beset by anxiety, along come our tenant farmers, from whom we expect payments in rice, to grumble about their poverty. Ah, to think people believe in paradise! Where? When? My one deathbed wish is that you not bury my coffin. Take it to the mountain and cremate it with no fuss. Doctor, please bear witness to my request. My last wish is that I not become like that Jōsuke of the Trance. Ah, everything is so tiresome. I don't want to say any more,' she said, closing her eyes and dying a moment later.

"In accordance with her last wishes, her body was brought to the mountain and cremated. Jōsuke of the Trance joined the tenant farmers and day workers, carried the coffin up the mountain, and until the coffin had been set on fire and the corpse had gone up in flames, and until the survivors had collected the tiny bones which remained among the ashes, he busied himself as a substitute cremator. But when people realized that his zeal was motivated only by his desire to get as much as possible for himself of the special dish of glutinous rice and black soybeans distributed to the mourners at ceremonies for the departed souls, they thought him mean spirited.

"'Forget about offering prayers to the Buddha to be reborn in the Land of the Lotus. Take a good look at what's happened to Jōsuke,' the villagers said, spitting at the mention of Jōsuke and admonishing their children not to follow his example. But some people said, 'That may be, but didn't Jōsuke come back to life and didn't he take a wife? This might very well be due to the beneficence of the Buddha, who wanted to fulfill a promise to him of a bond extending over two lifetimes between husband and wife.'

"Jōsuke's new wife—the former widow—sometimes got involved in knockdown domestic rows, after which she would always go running to her neighbors.

"'What have I done to deserve such a worthless fellow for a husband? Now I long for those days when I was a widow living on leftovers. Why doesn't my former husband come back to life again like this one has? If he were here, we wouldn't lack for rice or barley and we wouldn't be suffering without clothes on our backs as we are now,' she said, weeping openly in fits of regret.

"Many are the strange occurrences in this world."

When I finished taking notes, the brief winter sun had already gone down. The professor had overexerted himself; he looked tired. The book was open and spread out on his chest. He had shut his eyes under the faint yellowish lamplight. He did not offer criticisms or expound on his perceptions, which normally would have completed the session after such a story. When I thought about the hour or so it would take for me to get home, I felt impatient and, hastily saying good-bye, I left the professor's house.

Professor Nunokawa's house was in the outskirts of Nerima and in the fall many of the trees in this area scattered scarlet leaves on the ground. For someone like me who was from downtown Tokyo, the site evoked visions, tinged with nostalgia, of the Musashi plains. The bus route, however, was far off and to get to the station I had to walk quite a while through narrow paths made within fields which were occasionally surrounded by bamboo groves and forests. In summer and winter, this route was an arduous one. If I went the opposite way, I would come out on a highway and, even though the next station was a long distance away, I would be able to walk along a brightly lit row of houses.

But as I was accustomed to this other route, I had made it my routine to take the narrow paths in the fields even though it was dark. In the two or three days that had passed since I had last come, the daylight hours had grown shorter and I felt I should hurry. Burying my chin in the collar of my overcoat and holding my umbrella low, I walked along the dark path as a light rain started to fall.

Because I had not traded views with Professor Nunokawa about that strange man in "A Bond for Two Lifetimes," Jōsuke's lifelike figure came floating vividly into my consciousness as if he were there right before my eyes. In the story, there was no mention of Jōsuke as he had been before he had gone into a trance, only that in his next life he had changed into a stupid country bumpkin and had married into the family of a woman whose husband had died. It was not clear whether "A Bond for Two Lifetimes" derived from some specific source or was an imaginative creation of Akinari's later years.

But as Professor Nunokawa had stated, if the young Akinari of his thirties, the author of the gothic stories in *Tales of Moonlight and Rain,* had written this, he would have doubtless woven a tale of quite startling eroticism about a pious priest who was unable to get off the wheel of rebirth because, before going into his trance, he had looked at a beautiful woman and, his heart greatly moved, been doomed by that blind attachment to remain forever ringing the bell in his hand. In comparison to what the young Akinari might have produced, the Jōsuke of this "A Bond for Two Lifetimes" was so unkempt and stupid that, with only a slight shift, the whole incident could be transformed into vaudevillian comedy.

But the Akinari who had written this story must have already lost the sight in his left eye and his old wife, Sister Koren, probably had by then passed away. He must have been in an oppressed and isolated mood when he had composed this "Bond for Two Lifetimes." His tone half ridiculed and half feared those still smoldering, seemingly inextinguishable inner fires of sexual desire which were as strong as his creative impulses.

At the end of the story, he might have been trying to hint at the bizarre persistence of an old man's sexuality, which still squirmed about like maggots. Akinari's story told of a man who had once, perhaps, been a sage of high virtue and attained an enlightened understanding of the most crucial life-and-death matters. This man then had the unfulfilled sexual attachment of a former life finally satisfied through another woman's body, by returning to this world. This time, however, he had changed into an utter fool who could not comprehend a single letter.

The author displayed his skepticism twice in the story, when those old women, longing for their afterlife, mock the Buddhist laws of cause and effect. He seems to despise the very nature of sex, which goes endlessly around and around in a vicious cycle, never sublimated by old age or by devotion to religion.

This reminded me of Professor Nunokawa, who had taken in Mineko, so much younger than he. Stories were told about how she had already transferred ownership of the old house to her name, presuming the professor had not long to live. It was hard not to see similarities with Jōsuke's relationship with the widow.

While I was thinking over these matters, I suddenly had an unexpected remembrance of the last time I had embraced my husband, the night before he died in the bombing. I thought of how I had writhed in his strong arms, panting like a playful puppy, and had finally withered with the pleasures of a desire so strong that my body and soul seemed to have vanished. More than mere memory, those sensations suddenly all returned to my flesh. My very womb cried out in longing. A moment later, my foot slipped, I tottered two or three steps and seemed dangerously close to falling down on my knees.

"Careful," a man's voice said, taking hold of my arm, which was still clutching my umbrella. With his help, I managed to regain my feet.

"Thank you very much," I said, out of breath.

"Sometimes the bamboo roots stick out onto the road around here," the man said in a low voice and then asked, "Have you dropped anything?" and bent down to help me look.

He was right about where we were—on a path cut through a bamboo grove just halfway between the professor's house and the station; I could see the light from a house flickering through the thick stand of bamboo. I could not make out the man's face in the dark, and since he did not have an umbrella and his overcoat was wet, I asked him,

"Won't you come under?" and held out my umbrella. Without reserve, he brought his body right up against mine.

"Icy isn't it? And the rain makes it worse," he said, and with a chill ungloved hand, he gripped my hand to help me hold the umbrella.

Although I could not see his face clearly, from his voice and appearance he seemed rather old and shabby, yet the hand he put on top of my gloved one was soft like a woman's. I preferred men with strong, bony grips, just like my dead husband's and so I did not care for the softness of this man's. Strangely, I did not think of shaking him off and even felt the guilty pleasure of the cold softness of his palm slowly tightening around my glove. The man joined his outer hand to mine in carrying the umbrella and used the other hand to hold me around the shoulder. My body was completely encircled within his arms. We had to walk along entangled in this way.

In the darkness, I staggered frequently and each time he adjusted his hold on me, like a puppeteer manipulating a puppet. And, touching me on my breasts, my sides, and other parts of my body, he would laugh, but whether out of joy or sadness, I could not tell. I suddenly had the idea that he might be crazy, but that did not diminish the strange pleasure I took in his embrace.

"Do you know what I was thinking about when I slipped a minute ago?" I asked in a flirtatious voice that might have passed for drunkenness. He shook his head and embraced me so tightly that it became difficult to walk.

"I was thinking about my dead husband. He was killed by a bomb in an army air raid shelter in Kure. I was in a government housing area not very far away with our child and survived. You know, I wonder if my husband thought about me before he died. Now for some reason I long to know how he felt before he died. My husband loved me, but being a soldier, he made a distinction in his mind between loving and dying alone. I genuinely admire my husband's magnificent attitude toward life, but, up until the moment he died, did he really not see any contradiction between loving a woman and dying . . ."

The man did not answer my question, and as if to stop my words, he brought his cold lips against my mouth. Then, sadly rubbing my arms, he gave me a long kiss. As his cold tongue became intertwined with mine, his sharp teeth suddenly came against my tongue. They were unmistakably my husband's.

"Oh my dear, oh my dear, it's really you . . ." I called as the man pushed me down in the grove where the bamboo roots pressed hard against me, and then fell on top of me, all the while seeking my acquiescence. But his hands were indeed soft and cold, quite different from my husband's. Those hands groped over my prostrate form and, as I resisted, tried to undo the buttons of my overcoat. I called out weakly,

"I was wrong. You're not the one. You're not my husband."

He remained silent and, seizing one of my flailing hands, forced my fingers into his mouth. Behind his cold lips, his teeth were pointed, sharp awls, just like my husband's, which had passed painfully over my tongue so many times in the past. But the hands were different. My husband's hands had not been as fleshy and soft as a woman's. And his body also . . .

At that moment, I suddenly remembered the steamy, mildewed, invalid's smell I had confronted upon entering Professor Nunokawa's room. Was this Professor Nunokawa? The moment that idea crossed my mind, my voice called out totally different words, while my body sprang up convulsively like some stray dog.

"Jōsuke, Jōsuke! This is . . ."

Muttering these words, I ran full speed into the darkness.

When I emerged onto the brightly lit street in front of the station, my heart was still pounding from the vivid hallucination which had seized me on the dark path. A train had just arrived and a crowd of men in black overcoats on their way home from work came pushing their way out of the narrow ticket wicket, each looking as if he had been cast from the same mold. As I stood at the side of the wicket to let the group of men through, it occurred to me observing them, that each of them looked like an unimpeachably upstanding man. For me, a woman, they caused simultaneously a feeling of envy and a seering twinge . . .

I had ascertained that Jōsuke of the Trance was alive and well in these men. More than that embarrassing hallucination of what had gone on before on the dark path, this realization started my blood churning. It was an unsettling agitation that warmed my heart.

SIX POEMS

REINER KUNZE

Translated from the German by Lori M. Fisher

SUNDAY

1
Twenty centimeters above the knee

In stockings that
blossom above the thighs in
stockings branded like the snake in
invisible stockings knotted together like
rope ladders

2
The air above the sidewalks
vibrates from the clanging
of the abrupt bells

LIKE THINGS MADE OF CLAY

> *But i glue my halves together like a*
> *shattered pot made of clay*
> (Jan Skacel, letter of February 1970)

1
We wanted to be like things made of clay

To exist for those
who drink their coffee in the kitchen
at five in the morning

To belong to the simple tables

We wanted to be like things made of clay, made
of earth from the field

So no one could use us to kill

We wanted to be like things made of clay

In the midst of
       so much
           rolling
              steel

2
We will be like the fragments
of things made of clay: never again
whole, maybe
a flash
in the wind

SPEAKING TO RUSSIA

For Aleksandr Solzhenitsyn

Mother Russia, in the armpits
forests with elks and wolves

Your fine sons
praise you, raising their arms
almost to heaven

As if their words were
hobnails that they wanted to drive in
with bare fists

As if they nailed on their consciences
with iron persuasion

Self-conscious, they smile and
let their arms sink, i ask
about their brothers near your
heart

WITH THE VOLUME DOWN LOW

During those
twelve years
i was not allowed to publish says
the man on the radio

i think of X
and begin to count

TO YOU IN THE BLUE COAT

Once more I scan the row of houses
from the beginning searching for

you the blue comma that
gives meaning

REFUGE EVEN BEYOND THE REFUGE

For Peter Huchel

Here only the wind steps through the gate ininvited

Here
only god calls out

He orders infinite wires strung
from heaven to earth

From the roof of the empty stables
to the roof of the empty sheepfold
the torrent of rain
screeches out of the wooden gutter

What are you doing, asks god

Lord, i say, it
is raining, what
is one supposed to do

And his answer grows
green through all windows

CENTURIA

GIORGIO MANGANELLI

Translated from the Italian by Kathrine Jason

At approximately ten in the morning a bookish gentleman who suffered mild melancholia discovered the irrefutable proof of God's existence. The proof was complex, but not beyond the grasp of an average philosophical mind. The bookish man stayed calm. He read the proof over from end to beginning, sideways, beginning to end, and concluded that he had done a fine job. He closed his book of notes concerning God's undeniable existence and left the house to go about his business doing nothing—in other words, to live. At approximately four that afternoon on his way home, he realized that he had forgotten the exact phrasing of certain passages in the proof; and of course, they were all essential.

He was unnerved. He went into a bar for a beer, and he thought he felt calmer momentarily. He remembered one passage, but immediately two others slipped away. Perhaps there was hope in his notes, but he knew they were incomplete; he had left them that way precisely so that nobody, such as the maid, would be certain of God's existence before he had time to develop the entire argument meticulously. Two thirds of the way home he realized that while the proof was losing all its extraordinary distinguishing features, he was coming up against new arguments which probably had nothing to do with the original one. Had he written a passage about

Limbo? No, nor one about the Sleeping Souls, but perhaps he had written about the Last Judgment. He was not sure. And what about Hell? Probably not, yet he had the impression that he had pondered it at length, and that he had put Hell at the very top of his investigation. At his front door he broke into a cold sweat. He had proven the existence of something, but of what? Whatever had emerged was undoubtedly true and indisputable, but it could not be expressed in an unforgettable formula. Then and there he found himself clutching the keys to his house, and in a fit of delayed desperation, he flung them into the deserted street.

The gentleman wearing an overcoat with a fur collar, and a clean shave, left his house at exactly twelve minutes to nine, since at 9:30 he had a date with the woman to whom he will propose. Slightly behind the times, he is modest, serious, and reserved, not unsophisticated exactly, but a man whose frame of reference is deliberately outdated. He has decided to walk all the way to the appointment so that he has time to meditate, since he is sure that whatever the answer might be, his life is on the verge of a dramatic change. He expects a "maybe," so naturally he is apprehensive, though a "no" put kindly would overjoy him; he does not dare to consider an outright "yes." He has figured on a forty-minute walk, including time to buy the daily paper; chronicle of everyday brutality that it is, it convinces him of his own puniness. Since there are three possible answers, he has decided to devote a total of thirty minutes to the "no" and the "maybe," eight minutes to the "yes," and two to the newpaper.

Eight minutes into the walk, while trying to convince himself that a "no" would not keep him from living a useful and honest life, he heard the first violent explosion. It was true that according to recent rumors the time was ripe for a civil war in his country. But the gentleman wearing the overcoat, absorbed in his own future, had paid no attention. And even then he did not catch on. But two minutes later when he saw the Ministry of Education explode, he became suspicious. The tanks finally convinced him. His few political opinions were rather anemic, but thinking suddenly of his potential wife filled him with virile apprehension. Then things happened quickly: at 9:07 the prime minister was hurled from his office window, three minutes later the president was shoved down the chimney, and the king entered the Hall of Monarchs—he was old and in a hurry. The shootings began immediately afterward. They shot the man in the overcoat at 9:30 in front of the wall of a pseudo-Gothic church. They shot him holding the paper he had bought that morning, when the country was still a Republic. He did not mind dying, but those eight minutes he would have devoted to the "yes" nagged him.

Every day when he wakes up, which he does reluctantly, or better said, sluggishly, the gentleman starts the day with a quick inventory of the universe. He has understood for a time that although the Earth, his cockpit, has not noticeably changed, each day he wakens in a different spot in the cosmos. Ever since he was a child, he has been convinced that sometimes as the Earth moves space, it brushes by or actually enters Hell, though he has never had the chance to enter Heaven. Anything would certainly seem frivolous and laughable after that experience, and the world could not possibly carry on. So, it follows that Heaven must steer clear of the Earth at all costs so as not to upset creation's impeccable and incomprehensible design. Now as a grown man, the owner and driver of car, he still clings to that childish hypothesis though less fervently, and though his questioning is more metaphorical and detached. He knows that while he sleeps the whole Earth shifts—dreams prove it—and that every morning the Earth's pieces are rearranged, whether or not they are pawns in a game. He does not pretend to understand this shifting about, but he is sure that he senses presences which are sometimes abysses, sometimes cliffs that lure him, and more rarely, sprawling plains he longs to roll across for hours; and he fancies himself a round, celestial body. Occasionally he glimpses a blurred image of grasses, or has the exciting and usually not unpleasant sensation that several warring suns are illuminating him. Other times he finds himself listening to an uproar of waves so distinct, it could either be a storm or a lull. But then again, the most brutal revelation of all is his own position in the universe; for instance, the feel of cruel, eager jaws on the nape of his neck. His innumerable ancestors must have had the same sensation when they ended up between the teeth of that savage beast he has never seen head-on. It has been clear for some time that he never wakes up in his own room. In fact, he has concluded that the room does not exist, and that the walls and sheets are an illusion, a sham. He knows he is suspended in the void and that he, like everyone else, is the Earth's center, where infinite infinities begin. And this is too dreadful to bear, so he knows that the room, and even the abysses and Hell, were contrived to protect him.

At 10:30 in the morning, a fat, bearded gentleman wearing rumpled clothes realized he had the power to perform miracles. It required only the simplest gesture: running his right thumb along the tips of the index, middle, and ring fingers of the same hand. Naturally, the first time he had done it by chance and cured a languishing cat instantaneously. This was not "wish fulfillment," it was a miracle. But when he made that same gesture and asked a specific, yet reasonable sum of money nothing happened. He had to be doing a good deed. He cured a little boy, stopped a runaway horse, restrained a homicidal maniac, and kept a wall from toppling down on grandparents and tiny grandchildren. Sickening was the only word for it. He would have never believed that making miracles was such—what could you say?—such "cheap labor." The fat man had one and only one saving grace, but it was essential: he was not a believer. He was not an outright atheist because his was not a philosophical spirit, but religions, all of them, annoyed him. So why should this business of miracles have befallen him of all people? Supposing this proved the existence of some supreme power, what power was it? There were dozens of gods and demigods, demons, elves, and ghosts. He could not care less about performing miracles. So what was it, a prank? Upon the fortieth miracle he realized that word was getting around and decided to do something about it. And so he went to a neighborhood where he had never performed any miracles, and despite his qualms, entered the church and confronted the priest. He made it clear: not only that he was not a believer, but that his miracles might have been brought about by a completely different god than the one worshiped in that church. The priest did not seem astounded. "This is not the first case," he said, "but it has never happened to us here. You married?" "No." "Then why don't you become a priest?" "But I'm not a believer." "Who is these days? Look, you have a way with miracles; if it were mathematics I'd tell you to be an engineer." With his next-to-last miracle the fat man converted the priest and persuaded him to repent. With his last one he self-destructed to convince the priest that the previous miracle had actually happened. The experts really prized that final miracle.

That gentleman is plaster. Of course he is a monument. He could have been marble; but the city council chose plaster: it costs less. The plaster man is not offended. Plaster may not be resplendent, but it is dignified: it gets dirty, which is a sign of toil and day-to-day living—of a noble life. Being plaster, he probably has a family: a plaster wife in a park, a pair of plaster kids in a private garden or in the lobby of an orphanage. Marble statues do not have families. Marble is beautiful, its reflections are beautiful, and it is clean but so icy. No marble gentleman would have a woman, except in those unusual marriages arranged by the state, for the sake of the royal line. The plaster gentleman is rightly pleased with the way they have dressed him: the trousers tapered just so, smooth pocket flaps, jacket wrinkled as if a wind were blowing, a vest with all the buttons, of which he is very proud because a vest is a sign of a proper career. They have put a book under his right arm. He has no idea what book it is—the title is facing the street so that people can read it. Actually, nobody except some dawdling child ever reads it. He does not know what the book is about, or whether it is his or just on loan. Not being able to read the title bothers him, so he tries to read the children's smooth lips but never succeeds. And there's another detail that rather annoys him: he is standing— he realizes there are seated statues, but that does not bother him— on a base with something written on it. It must be a name and the dates of birth and death. He is a monument, so he does not care about the dates, but he does care about the name of the man whose monument he is.

He is perfectly happy to be the monument, but couldn't they tell him whose? Fine, the important thing is to be a good monument, to enjoy the pigeons fluttering around him. The monument does not know, however, that the gentleman whose monument the plaster gentleman is, is furious. Him and his plaster! Him and his pigeons! With *that* book under his plaster arm, when he has written so many other, greater, even more definitive ones! The gentleman is infuriated, but he did always have a horrible personality anyway. He has not passed through these parts since he died, some twenty years ago. But during gusty rainstorms, he emerges from a little side street, hoping to see the plaster gentleman go to pieces, melt! Him and his birdshit! What a pity no one ever tells him how glad the plaster gentleman is to be his monument, he and his wife, Cleo, muse of History.

This place is not exactly human: its inhabitants are not human beings. In fact they have strange notions about men that ancient storytellers passed down and that merchants, geographers, and forgerers of photographs invented. The more educated among them do not believe in human beings at all. They say it is all just an old and utterly preposterous superstition; actually, the belief is limited to the lower classes. Children believe in them too, thus, a complex mythology with human characters has arisen. In these tales, the people do funny, and in their peculiar way, sinister things, such as devising rational yet unreasonable plots. But the most strange and colorful outgrowth of the human tradition is the mask and puppet industry. Valuable objects are produced and sold, not only for children's amusement, but also for decoration in the apartments and homes of the educated, who do not believe in people. Naturally, the masks and puppets are not exact replicas since a human has never been seen and may not even exist. Therefore they rely on the traditions of old ridiculous books with illustrations, and finally, on their imagination. The human face always has holes for seeing, usually two, placed haphazardly, one on top and one at the bottom or in the middle—on the belly. The human's upper portion is round or square, and another part with limbs for taking and walking is attached to it. To communicate he emits sounds from somewhere or other—and this is where the artists let their imaginations run wild. Some draw trumpets sprouting straight out of the head, or else a series of holes, like those on a flute or ocarina. To listen he has a fleshy sort of orifice which can appear on various parts of the body. The puppets of supposedly "sick people" are favorites, as difficult as it is to imagine the illnesses of imaginary beings. Some are covered with sores and boils, and secrete vital fluids, while some cannot see through their holes; others have decrepit flutes that make no sounds or limbs that cannot touch, grab, or move. Still, there are those who theorize that human beings are immortal and show these masks great respect. But should they ever find a mask unworthy or irreverent, they burn it in sacrifice.

For a couple of days he has been very uneasy. After a long, solitary life, he realizes that his apartment is inhabited by other beings. Three ghosts, two fairies, a spirit, a devil, and a huge angel who takes up a whole room by himself have set up housekeeping in the three rather bizarre rooms of his house. He suspects there might be others too—round, miniscule beings that he cannot name. This sudden influx disturbs him. He cannot understand why all these beings have chosen his house. Are they there for some reason? The worst of it is, they refuse to come out, to talk or communicate with him in any way, even in sign language. He cannot go on living in a house infested like this; if he could just speak to these images, he might make sense of their strange occupancy, and perhaps find meaning in his own life too. There's no actual way to prove that the beings are in the house, nonetheless their presence is not only obvious but nerve-wracking. He has tried to convince them to appear, appealing to each of the three ghosts individually, and even suggesting that they make a racket, terrify the whole neighborhood. When no one broke the silence, he turned to the devil, known for his professional inclination for conversation. He was deliberately vague about his own soul when alluding to a bargain, hoping either to lure the devil out, or at least to irritate the angel. No answer. So he scattered flowers around the house to attract the fairies. To invoke the spirit he used a foolproof method. Actually, the beings crowding every corner of his house want nothing to do with him. Only the little spheres are polite—now and then he hears them buzzing briefly in his ears. But he should only know that the three ghosts, two fairies, and spirit are waiting for the next tenant to move in after his demise, which is imminent. The angel and devil are ready to tend to the bureaucracy. And in a distant city, the future tenant is already packing his suitcases, frantically leaving a house infested by spirits.

One day an illustrious bell maker with a long beard, a confirmed atheist, was visited by two customers. They were dressed in black, seemed very serious, and had a swelling at their shoulders, which the atheist thought might have been wings—like the ones angels supposedly have. But his convictions led him to dismiss this. The two gentlemen commissioned the master to make a huge bell out of an alloy he had never used before, nor had he ever worked in such great dimensions. The gentlemen explained that the bell would produce a unique sound, unlike any other's. Then, as they were leaving, the two explained with some embarrassment that this bell would be used at the hour of the Last Judgment, which was already imminent. The master chuckled and said there would never be a Last Judgment, but added that he would finish the bell to their liking by a certain day.

The gentlemen stopped by every two or three days to see how the work was progressing. They were a gloomy pair, and even though they praised the master's work, they seemed secretly dissatisfied. Then for a while, they did not come at all. Meanwhile, the master completed the greatest bell of his life, and feeling great pride, realized that in his heart of hearts he wished that such a bell, the only one of its kind, could be used at the hour of the Last Judgment. When the bell had been finished and mounted on a great wooden platform, the two men reappeared. They gazed at the bell admiringly, yet in despair. They sighed. Finally, the one who seemed the more authoritative, turned to the master and muttered, almost in shame: "Master, you were right. There will not be a Last Judgment, not now or ever. We've made a terrible mistake." The master looked at the two gentlemen kindly. He too was sad, yet he seemed content. "Too late, my friends," he said in a low, contained voice. Then, giving the cord a tug, the bell rocked and tolled, tolled loud and clear. And as they should have, the heavens parted.

The knight who slayed the dragon, a handsome, slender, neat man of great bearing—though admittedly mortal—yokes the grisly slab of flesh to his saddle and sets out on the road for the city. He is proud of his undertaking though he somehow suspects that his arrow was guided by equal strokes of fate and stupidity. When he passes through villages, the townsfolk, who are accustomed by now to the horrifying monster, shut themselves in their houses and bar the doors. The knight laughs, thinking that when he gets to the city the king will embrace him before all the people and offer his daughter's hand in marriage, out of decorum, if nothing else. Dragging the dragon's body, its teeth and half-closed eyes behind him, the knight passes a church, a cemetery, and a solitary house. But no one appears to pay him respect, not even the dead whose whispering could even be a reproach. Why doesn't the priest come out to bless the killer? Why don't the people who live in that house come out to kiss his stirrups? Can they be afraid of the very man who liberated them from the horrible monster? The knight is infuriated, and all the more proud of his undertaking. Here he comes, passing through the city gates, moving along the great street toward the palace; the street is crammed, but as he presses onward, he senses something strange happening: as the crowd falls silent and withdraws, he realizes that they are not averting their eyes from the horrible monster, but from him, the knight. He has to acknowledge the sense of repulsion growing around him—the townsfolk are not just afraid, they are repelled. The knight is shocked, indignant, exhausted. A window shuts matter-of-factly, he thinks he hears a quick fire of insults. But didn't he kill the dragon? Didn't everyone agree that the dragon should have been killed? Wasn't history full of paladins who had slain dragons and won women and Japanese motorcycles? Could he have killed the wrong dragon? No, no one had ever mentioned two dragons; there weren't two, absolutely not. He should be furious, but he is only downcast. He doesn't understand. He realizes now that it would be pointless to go to the king, so he stops at a crossroad, and the people draw back. What to do? The knight dismounts and turns to look at the ugly, motionless dragon. For the first time he scrutinizes its body, face, tough skin, and stiff spikes. And what does the knight feel? For the first time he is afraid, and he sees that his destiny as a dragon-slayer is laughable, villainous. And confused, he realizes that he will spend the rest of his life contemplating that indestructible corpse.

He often wonders if the problem of his relationship with the sphere is not inherently unresolvable. He cannot always see the sphere, but even when he leaves, moves away or hides from it, the sphere reacts. He realizes the universe is designed to accommodate the sphere. Sometimes waking in the half-darkness of his room—the day has already begun, but he is not a late sleeper so much as an oversleeper—he sees the sphere hovering in the middle of the room. He observes it carefully, for it requires attention like a question. The sphere is not always the same color, but fades from black to gray. Sometimes, and this upsets him, it turns inside out, so that a round cavity, an utterly lightless void, takes its place. Sometimes it is gone for days, even ten. Then it comes back suddenly, without rhyme or reason, when he least expects it, as if it were returning from a trip, a prearranged yet suspect absence. Then the sphere pretends to be apologetic, but is actually being ironic and vicious, even if unwittingly. Once he resorted to violence trying to wipe that repulsive presence out of his life. But the sphere is silent and elusive except before it strikes: then it inflicts an opaque, deep, rending pain where it touches the body. The sphere's most typical act of hostility is to get in the way and block out something he wants to see: it sometimes shrinks to minute proportions like a slippery little ball bobbing before his eyes. Still, as if he did not know the sphere was utterly indestructible, he longs for a sudden, brutal confrontation. Sometimes he thinks of escaping, starting his life over in a place the sphere does not know. But this will not work. He knows he will have to talk the sphere out of existence, seduce it slowly toward nothingness. And that labyrinthine journey takes time, patience, cunning.

TWO POEMS

LÊDO IVO

Translated from the Brazilian Portuguese by Kerry Shawn Keys and John M. Tolman

LUNCH PAIL

In his lunch pail
the worker
carries absolutely no metaphysics.
He carries fried fish,
rice and beans.
In his lunch pail
everything has its place.
Everything is limited
and nothing is infinite.
The water cup
has space only
for his thirst.
And the lunch pail is the same
as the mouth of his stomach,
made to order

for his hunger.
And when he finishes
his lunch
he stubbornly hunts
all the crumbs,
all the oil
that a piece of bread
sweats during working hours.
All that he earns
the worker applies
like capital
to his lunch pail.
And what he doesn't earn
although he works
is another kind of capital
that he also invests:
the words he says
in the union hall,
the sentence written
on the factory wall,
a vision of the future
born in his eyes
that only fill with tears
from the smoke stacks.
In his lunch pail
the worker carries
no caviar of
any sort of metaphysics.
And, he, being the most
exact of men,
everything about him is physical
and material,
it has its name and form,
its weight and volume,
it can be touched.
His love has a skirt
hair and mucous membranes
and, fertile, makes
new workers.

Things are measured
by their size:
sleep, table, rafter.
On the train or the bus
no worker
can stretch
without an effort.
Just like the world:
one must push.
Chock-full
of the right material,
his life is exact
like a lunch pail.
His whole life
fits it perfectly.
Death doesn't fit
because it doesn't exist,
not being manual,
not being a thing to patch
(An infinite article,
without iron, without steel,
anybody can wrap it up
without using string
or wrapping paper.)
Industrial and essential
the worker lives
from what he knows and does
and, being alive,
he inhales what he sees.
Time that dirties him
with oil and soot
also washes him,
time made of water
open in the afternoon,
not that of clocks.
And the lunch pail itself
is also washed.
And when he takes it
home with him,

the metal smells
less of food
than it does of him.

THE GATE

The gate is open all day long
but at night, I myself go to close it.
I expect no nocturnal visitor
except the thief who jumps over the wall of dreams.
The night is so quiet that it makes me hear
the birth of fountains in the forests.
My bed, white as the Milky Way,
is too small for me in the black night.
I occupy all the space in the world. My distracted hand
knocks down a star and frightens a bat.
The beating of my heart fascinates the owls
in the branches of the cedars, pondering the mystery
of day and night, born of the waters.
In my stonelike sleep I stay still and travel.
I am the wind that caresses artichokes
and rusts the harness hanging in the stable.
I am the ant that, guided by the constellations,
breathes the perfume of land and sea.
A man who dreams is everything that he isn't:
the sea that ships have damaged,
the black whistle of the train passing through trestles,
the soot that darkens the kerosene drum.
If I shut my gate before I sleep,
in dreams it opens itself. And he who didn't come during the day,
stepping on dry eucalyptus leaves,
comes at night and knows the way, like the dead,
who haven't yet come, but know where I am,
covered by a winding sheet, like all who dream
and stir in the darkness, and shout the words
that escaped the dictionary and went to smell

the night air scented with jasmine and sweet, fermenting manure.
The undesirable visitors cross through the locked doors
and the Venetian blinds that filter the passage of the breeze,
and encircle me.
Oh, mystery of the world! No lock shuts the gate of night.
In vain at nightfall I thought to sleep alone
protected by the barbed wire that circles my fields
and by my dogs that dream with open eyes.
At night, a simple breeze destroys the walls of men.
Although my gate will be locked in the morning,
I know that someone opened it in the silence of night,
and, in the darkness, watched over my restless sleep.

THE CONFESSIONS OF FRIDAY

JAMES B. HALL

Those Island memories of Order and Innocence fade now with my waning Sexuality and from the increased burthen of this, my Publik House. Sole proprietor of this Flute & Cobbler, my mirrored, well-lighted cubicles above-stairs for your Pleasures, without Rancour, and now called Jas. Friday, I live on. Even so, I understand an Island held now only in Memory, held while ironshod carriage wheels outside echo in the fogs of the Thames and then re-echo along the stone alleyways of London, well signifies the True Nature of our Lives.

It is almost Winter, past Noon; my accounts are to-date, my desk lamp burns. In the centre of a lamp's flame again, I see the Sun rise in those Savage latitudes of the River Oronoque. Once I lived there. I elected to depart.

All the more odd, his storybook, his so-called novel, his *Life and Strange Surprizing Adventures of Robinson Crusoe, Mariner York* is still believed, is still read by certain Gentlemen. For those lies, those perversions, I told one Defoe, Dissenter, sometimes Sectarian Preacher, solely responsible. The man's a scoundrel, an opportunist: he dare not set one foot in my Flute & Cobbler.

About that footprint. My own footprint discovered in the sand: Oh, that footprint is now most celebrated, is said to be a "high moment in our literature." In fact, one day past Noon, in the sand by the water's edge, I *arranged* for Crusoe to discover it.

From the very beginning I was also on that Island—*our* Island.

R. Crusoe was the first man into the lifeboat after our Ship wrecked in the great Storm. The boat swamped and Crusoe was swept ashore. Commonly, it is said, Crusoe was saved by holding fast to a rock; I happen to know he was saved by a Ship's plank, random in the Seas.

But I, Jas. Friday, also came ashore in that blackest night buoyed only by the wave's force to which I abandoned myself without either thought or plan—for such was my Nature. I held no rock; I rode no plank. Yet I, too, survived.

Continually, R. Crusoe bleats of "Providence," but that night our difference was only in degree, in the colour of our skin. Our feet found identical Salvation on sand. So I ask you: "Whose Providence?"

Here are the Facts. Judge for yourself.

Before dawn of that first day, already awake, I was cross-legged, facing East to watch the gigantic head and shoulders of the Sun vault skyward to become the first dawn of this, my new, my liberated Life. In wonder, I gazed across the illuminated swells of the Sea. Through mists, intermittently, as though in a Vision, I glimpsed the high stern, the wreck of the *Albion Castle;* in sunlight, in calmer Seas, the Ship was but two leagues offshore. I observed that wreck only as a distant Curiosity.

Well-refreshed by sleep, with no care for the Future, I went singing along the beach. The tide incoming filled my footprints as I walked.

Beyond the next point of land, I discovered one Robinson Crusoe.

I bent closer, the better to see Crusoe's face. In this day's first heat, his body and his bodyrags gave off an offensive odor. As Crusoe breathed, he seemed to sink deeper into the sand. One unnaturally white, exposed arm still clutched a Ship's plank; by contrast, my own black, naked arm was supple, alive. For one moment I feared this man.

Aboard the *Albion Castle* (6 guns, 14 men), Crusoe was not well respected. In Storms he was pious, but in good weather bullied all persons of "lower" social order than himself. Because I was black and our dear Captain's boy (slave), Crusoe did not conceal a Malevolence towards me and all my kind.

Treacherous, a hardened seafarer, once a captive of the Moors, Crusoe boasted incessantly of Profits taken from voyages past. On his trowser belt, Crusoe carried always his knife in a leather sheath. With satisfaction, I saw this identical sheath still in place, now filled with sand.

My moment of Fear passed as the shadow of a gull's wing skims the sand: my emotions were neither long nor very deep, for such is my Nature. To kill Crusoe where he lay did not cross my Mind; instead, I was overwhelmed with Joy to know we were now equals, were not alone on this desperate Island. R. Crusoe was now my Fellow Man: with that clear recognition, the final vestige of slave-mentality passed from my Life.

Flies buzzed at Crusoe's eyelids. For the joke of it—just for play—I dribbled a handfull of sand near the fly-blown mouth. Crusoe twitched. Violently, he rolled his head. In sleep Crusoe called out for his mother.

I departed. On a low dune, not thirty feet above him, I blended into the vines, the leaves. An audience of one, as though looking down into a sunlit Theatre, I observed R. Crusoe, Mariner York, awake.

Crusoe shook my sand from his beard, his hair, from his rags; he stooped on all fours, then stood erect.

Crusoe walked a few paces one way, then another, as though still confined to a Ship's deck. He raised both arms to Heaven, stared briefly into the tropik Sun. Overly long, he gazed across the now-calm Sea: in a slanting ray of the Sun, glistening off-shore like a jewel in the black fist of the reef, Crusoe saw the wreck of the *Albion Castle* (120 tons, 14 men). As he watched, entranced, a long comber broke as spray across the bulwarks of that wreck.

Crusoe cried out. He called each name of the fourteen (white) crewmen; he shouted for Van Dryssen, our old Dutch Captain, lately my dear Master. No one answered. Behind me, surprized by that hoarse, strange voice, a massive flock of sea birds rose flapping.

Crusoe kneeled in sand, sobbed as a child. With the hectoring voice of the bully, Crusoe prayed. Neither Sea nor sand nor sea birds made reply.

At that moment of unrequited Silence, I felt great Compassion for R. Crusoe, Castaway.

Finally, Crusoe turned his back on the Sea. He stood not twenty paces from where I lay among vines. From fern leaves and fronds, Crusoe fashioned a conical hat; he placed it on his head as protection from the Sun. Savagely, he broke down a small tree, and got himself a staff, a walking stick. With his new hat and cane, and with new Determination, Crusoe turned again to the shore.

I laughed and laughed: Crusoe had walked along my own footprints in the sand, footprints which lead directly to my place of hiding. But Crusoe saw them not. Being now Castaway by "Providence," Crusoe saw himself as utterly alone; therefore, he saw and could see only those things which confirmed his new Role.

The Sun was directly overhead. I gathered a few berries within reach. In the first hot hours of the day, I felt my natural Indolence assert itself; I felt myself become at one with the rhythm, with the Life of another Island, an order of things felt but not seen.

Towards evening I awoke. Crusoe was gone. I remembered the Savagery with which Crusoe attacked the defenseless tree to get him a walking stick; therefore, I was at pains to keep from his sight. I became a shadow moving through the undergrowth, so quiet even shore birds fed undisturbed.

Not far from the place Crusoe had prayed in the sand, I found a pile of things he had gathered on a long beach patrol. He had arranged this Debris in a precise order: three hats, one cap, and two shoes which were not fellows. Crusoe's crude monument signified the end of my dear Captain, his crew, and of their enterprise to take slaves in Africa.

More importantly, Crusoe was now returning from his first trip to the wreck of the *Albion Castle*.

From the bush above a small inlet, I watched Crusoe's new raft run aground on a sandbar beyond the mouth of the creek. The raft was made of Ship's spars, was cumbersome—and loaded with goods. With his stick, Crusoe tried to free the raft and its cargo. Then with a boat hook from the wreck, he punched violently at the water. He cursed. In desperation, Crusoe finally jumped overboard. Without his weight, the raft unexpectedly broke free of the sand. Wind and tide at once pushed his raft back towards the ocean.

Crusoe swam in chase. He managed to catch the end of a line which bound the Ship's spars. Crusoe knotted the line around his shoulders. Steadily he swam. Then, hysterically, he threw his arms at the water—made no headway. Crusoe became weaker, gave up. He tried to regain the low-riding raft but was too weak. Raft and man drifted steadily seaward.

I stood. I was at the point of rescuing Crusoe, our raft, and our first cargo from the *Albion Castle*. Whereupon an afternoon inshore breeze came up. Our raft began to drift once again towards the inlet. Crusoe was strong enough to guide the raft, but not more. In half an hour, man and raft drifted ashore about twenty yards below me. Exhausted, Crusoe lay himself athwart our "goods," more dead than alive.

I waited, concealed, until Crusoe slept. For the second time that day I observed Crusoe snoring.

Again, I might have killed him, but—childlike—was eager to see the goods which Crusoe fetched us from the wreck: . . . One chest carpenter's tools. Four pieces dried goat's flesh. One Dutch cheese, rind broken. Four demijohns Cordial Waters. Most fearful: two pistols, two large powder horns, one bag shot; two fowling pieces; also two swords, handguards rusty. The twenty powder kegs aboard were still dry and waited in the reared aft-cabins.

Closely I inspected this mixed Cargo. I liked the Cordial Waters and one cheese with a broken rind; the iron things, the armament, I understood not at all.

And, of course, I saw it very well. While I slept, Crusoe laboured: from Piety he had gathered the Debris of the dead, including two shoes not fellows; that done, he had risked his Life to gain the wrecked Ship on the reef. For that risk had got him two swords, pistols, shot, powderhorns, fowling pieces.

Then, sadly, I understood: early we two had been free, innocent; this Island, this new World had been before us. With fowling pieces ashore, however, Crusoe need place one hand on his pistol and once more I became a slave, his slave.

Alone, Crusoe severed our natural Dependency, one man upon the other. In so doing, Crusoe divided our Island unequally: my island against His Island. These things I saw, but held no hard feelings: if to be armed was Crusoe's Nature, our stay on this Island was only beginning.

Therefore, I turned away, deserted Crusoe where he slept. I walked South along the water's edge, and the Tide closed my footprints. At a distance, abruptly, I turned East. My half of this Island lay across an interior spine of hills. Wind among stones taller than my head made the noise of wild beasts; as I walked more quickly, even the ferns hissed. I was a dark shadow in motion through dark hills.

At dawn, I emerged from trees. I saw our Island's other shore, there to live in ways most suited to my Nature.

Without plan, without Thought, each season passed, each season's end marked by the bloom and the decay of a bush-like yellow flower. Twice each year rain became incessant, went then back to the Sea. My half of the Island was a Paradise of Innocence; here time itself was lost, for I neither changed nor seemed to grow older. Of Crusoe, of his schemes, I gave no thought. Each night, overhead, the Southern Cross swung low in steady orbit.

Two years passed.

Each tree held parrots, their wings blue and orange among green leaves. Fish entrapped themselves in tidepools, and when I stooped to see my own reflection in the water, of Curiosity, the fish swam into my hands. I saw Ground Hares, pigeons, tortoise, and goats with their young; yet, with berries sweet in all seasons, with Food everywhere, I took only tortoise eggs or fruit. I neither fished nor stored meats against Famine; I killed no living thing and yet that Land fed me.

Four years passed.

Of clothing, I had none. My skin turned dark in Summer, became less so in the two seasons of rain when I slept much among fronds in my dry cave. By Chance one day, I covered my Body randomly with wet, scarlet leaves. As I lay in the sun, I felt the wet leaves suck my skin. When I removed the leaves, my skin was bleached in leaf-patterns of white. I was delighted. For days, I covered my Body with leaf-shapes. By arranging small leaves on my skin, I came to resemble a vine, a palmetto, or even the shell of a tortoise. Decorated artfully, I blended perfectly with flowers. At last my blackness was nullified. I became all things, a creature without qualities.

And I was young, my Sexuality not yet waning. When the Impulse seized me—which was often—I visited one of my six forked tree branches, all at least thirty feet above the ground. These forks I lined with moss, then laved them with wild-bee honey. These tree forks I embraced. In Extasy I tossed wildly in the sea winds. I reached Climax. Then I slept while the breeze rocked both the sweet, moss-lined fork and my limp Body . . .

Eight years passed.

One day at Noon, my skin dappled, I rose from sleep among the yellow flowers, those blossoms already decayed, for this was a season's end.

Offshore, all in a row, coming rapidly towards me, I saw five *canoes*. They converged. The black oarsmen leaped out; they beached the hulls. Only then, on the breeze, I heard the voices: the shouts of Savages—what? Come to take me?

Forty-one spear-armed men at once began to work: one group dug a deep hole in the sand; others ran the beach to get firewood. In headdress-feathers and calico, their drums beating a slow frenzy, the Chiefs of this war party danced on one foot around and around the hole in the sand.

A single, wood-gathering Savage came inland, paused not ten paces away; he was five feet three or four inches in height, a white animal bone skewed through the nose; the forehead, cheeks, arms, and smooth, perspiring chest were tattooed most intricately with purple dye. My own skin blended perfectly with the yellow flowers. The fearful Savage walked on.

Their fire on the beach burned brighter. Soon the blacks circled around and around two men whom I had thought were motionless Priests. Then I understood: the two moved not, because they were bound with ankle cords. From behind, without Warning, the two bound men were struck. Fell. Were killed instantly by warclubs.

I watched. Fascinated, the black Savages cut out the guts, then cut off the heads, the arms, the limbs, all the while shouting with Joy. When that awful Meat was broiled, they ate. Last, and apparently with especial relish, they passed, one to the next, the two roasted Hearts. Each Savage—without reluctance—ate his cooked share.

If fascinated, I was also sickened. If motionless, I was also relieved. They did not yet know of my Presence—or did they? Continuously, four dogs, tied by ropes to the canoes, lunged and barked in my direction.

The blacks were a war party. They had taken two prisoners. But when not at war, at some precise phase of the Moon, would they return for me? I presumed so.

My only thought was Flight.

Through those next hours, I trembled beneath palm fronds in my Cave. Incessantly, I thought of Robinson Crusoe. I saw myself warning Crusoe of Savage boat crews, of their dogs lunging at the underbrush; I would throw myself at his feet, give myself to him, claim him my Protector—for such was my Nature.

Dawn turned my Cave's mouth purple, then orange. I rose, and at once ran away between tall rocks, ran West beneath thwarted trees.

Past sunrise, after eight years of Innocence, again I saw the austere, rocky coast of Crusoe's Island. The inlet and the creek below had not changed; on the distant reef no sign remained of the *Albion Castle*. All was quiet, as though his half of the Island were suspended in the early morning sunshine between Sky and Sea. *Then I heard a musket shot.* The noise of a fowling piece re-echoed from a nearby gully, and I heard the cries of sea birds, the panic of wings beating. Crusoe was shooting his breakfast.

Cautiously, I walked towards the noise: because Crusoe's guns were in order, I was less afraid. Suddenly I drew back. My vine-leafed skin blended perfectly with the underbrush. Crusoe was walking this same path—not twenty paces away.

He wore a conical, peaked hat of the whitest goatskin, the rim broad against the tropik Sun. Over each shoulder was a fowling piece. From Crusoe's belt hung one of the swords, its handguard now brightly shining; his doublet and trowsers were of fine skins. On his belt, I saw the sheath of leather, a knife snuggly fitted, its handle of shaped horn. From his gun barrels hung four birds, maimed, bleeding.

Sturdy, stooped, a little fat, Crusoe came towards me. His face and his expressionless blue eyes thrust forward beneath the conical hat, as though he were moving at great speed. Crusoe loomed large, then passed my bush—an apparition in goatskin.

In eight years, I had seen no other civilized Person. And oh, I felt a great rush of Affection for I was Emotion's child. Yet I hesitated, drew back: if Crusoe and his guns signified my protection, those things also signified Oppression, the shackles of iron, the color of my skin.

Therefore, in the weeks ahead, from vines, from aloft in trees, at times standing not ten paces away, I observed Robinson Crusoe's every move. At sunup he arose, kneeled in prayer; daily he importuned—or threatened—a God who had either saved or had abandoned him. Prayers done, Crusoe talked aloud to himself all the day, a Habit engendered by his own years of isolation. At first I enjoyed the sound of his voice: to me it was a half-remembered Human Musick.

Unwittingly, inevitably, Crusoe told me everything: his present fears, his future plans for his New Order in part already imposed upon these stones. If Crusoe was his own Grand Architect, sole audience, and only consumer, he was at the same time both devious and cunning. If Crusoe's life was predictable and boring, I also laughed to observe him set little deadfalls and security-traps which he, himself, then must remember and later avoid. On his side of our Island, everywhere, there were now monuments to his Intellect, his Industry.

Central to Crusoe's New Order was The Cave. Here his wealth was stored. With its corridors, its propped, dug-out rooms, The Cave was at the Island's highest point. Often when Crusoe was at hunt, I, too, avoided his elaborate little traps. I, myself, constantly explored his most sacred Cave.

Beyond his storerooms I came upon a startling, isolated, cubicle: here was Crusoe's clepsydra, his water clock. This ingenious, altar-like construction was a glass demijohn from the wreck, the glass pierced artfully to allow water, drop-by-drop-by-drop, to escape into a bowl of brass. By trial and error Crusoe had marked the bowl with Roman numerals. All through the days and nights the water drop-dropped, and in this way Crusoe had mastered Time, had contained it.

A connected, adjacent room was Crusoe's "Academy of Weights and Measures." Here he had contrived the measure of an inch, a foot, a yard, a rod; likewise, a gill, a pint, two pecks, a gallon, a dram, and one pound avoirdupois. All models were of laboriously polished granite or the hardest of cured woods. These artifacts I understood to be the instruments, the weapons, of Reason.

Deeper in The Cave, connected and reached by short tunnels, were Crusoe's "Court of Justice," and its nearby jail. By chance, later, I discovered a trap door, and a smaller, deeper chamber. Here Crusoe had built a rack, stocks, and a modest gallows; also, with less care, he had assembled a brutally heavy, crude cross of oak. At these things, and more, I stared in wonder.

Well enough, however, I understood these Monuments were crude extensions of Crusoe's logical, mercantile, ranging Mind. Moreover, these things were most surely built against the day another storm wreck of mariners or slaves en route from Africa might come ashore to populate Crusoe's imagined "Kingdom."

Well enough, also, I understood myself to be Crusoe's best chance to get him at least one Citizen—albeit black—to govern.

In the domestic reaches of The Cave, I viewed rude bags of seed grains, dried goat's meat on hooks; tools, weapons, two chests, fine clothes; one chest, Gold. The Gold I marked well, but saw no way to get it for myself.

Into what I believed to be The Cave's deepest reach, Crusoe withdrew for solace, for meditation. In a soundless chamber, lined with pillows, an intricate woven canopy overhead, in this dark place which was so feminine, so maternal, Crusoe allowed but two furnishings. On the one hand, was an altar, and the Bible, a relick of a Ship once wrecked on that distant reef. On the other hand, in the center of a ring of pillows, was an elaborate Hooka, an intricately constructed water pipe. Once each month, Crusoe allowed himself to smoke one ounce of his precious, remaining Tobacco.

This dark, clandestine, room—and the Hooka pipe—at once became my Obsession. While Crusoe repaired his irrigation system for the rice paddies or sorted and numbered his goats, all through the hottest hours of every possible day, I came here. Without restraint, greedily, I smoked Crusoe's precious Sot Weed. I liked to watch the changing shapes, the patterns of my Smoke as it rose to the ceiling of the Cave. All ashes, all evidence, I swept carelessly into what I presumed was a well in the corner of the room.

Then one day, bored, careless, under the influence of the rising coils of Smoke, I lay alone in the centre of this most feminine of chambers. I slept.

Suddenly I awoke. I heard the clatter of deadfalls, of gates, of a goat herd bleating. Crusoe was here: had returned unexpectedly. A summer Storm—and lightning—was driving him headlong into our Cave.

Terrified, I picked up the water pipe. I threw the Hooka, lighted, into the well. I crouched. I ran on all fours along the chamber walls. I was trapped.

Eyes half-closed from rain, half-blinded by lightning, Crusoe could not see clearly. We passed, almost touched in the corridor. If he half-glimpsed me, Crusoe must have thought I was a goat. Sideways, I threw myself into the jail-room.

At that moment *there was an enormous Explosion,* bouncing me against the wall. Livid flame rushed like an orange wind from The Cave, showing—like the noon Sun—Crusoe appearing to lean forward into the flame. Then he was lifted up, thrown back, as though hurled from a cannon. I saw him outlined: a flapping ragdoll against The Cave's mouth.

Deeper in The Cave, I heard timber-props and walls let go. Because I was in the most protected room, I lay unharmed. I ran for the Entrance. Behind me, coming closer, I heard slabs of rock coming down . . .

I understood: when I threw away the Hooka pipe, it landed not in a well but in Crusoe's powder magazine!

Outside, blown clear of The Cave's mouth, I found Robinson Crusoe. I bent above his singed, smouldering beard. Clothing asunder, not conscious, Crusoe curled on the mossy roots of a rubber tree as though in sleep.

I felt great Remorse. Oh, so very much, I regretted my Sloth, my aimless self-centered Life which led to this wanton Destruction. For the pleasure of watching rings of Smoke, I had obliterated Crusoe's labours, his dreams of Governance. His beard still smouldered. I poured water on his poor, flame-ravaged face.

About me I saw two split baskets, two muskets, their barrels twisted; the Weights and Measures now rubbish; his Calendar Mast on fire; two goats burned terribly and crying; garments burning, two split sacks of rice. And over everything, the industrial, knife-sharp odour of Gunpowder.

And yet, Crusoe breathed.

To give Crusoe new Hope, to redress the Wrong I had done him, to reform my Life, to make Amends, the very next day I watched until Crusoe waded into the saltwater of the Sea to treat his powder-burns. When Crusoe was waist-deep in water, as he stared with longing at an empty Sea, I walked openly to the beach, to the shoreline.

Knowing well that in this dazed, timeless state, he must now observe it, must be astounded, knowing well he must now embrace me as an equal, I left that single—and that now *so* famous—footprint in the sand.

Crusoe came ashore.

As I had arranged from the beginning, Crusoe stared, then shouted for Joy. He fell on his knees in Prayer, and I stood beside him.

I placed my hand on Crusoe's shoulder. At the touch of my hand, Crusoe turned, saw me. Despite his ruined, blackened face, Crusoe almost smiled.

"You . . . You!" he said, for to Crusoe's mind I was not so much a person as I was his own Prayers answered. If at that moment Crusoe thought I was a Savage, a mindless thing, I was also a Man.

"You," Crusoe said. Then he strengthened. In his old voice of command he said: "I name you . . . Friday. James Friday."

And so I have been called to this very day.

Of my Life with Crusoe those next eight years, little more needs be said. If Crusoe built first an elaborate, rational Empire in his own image, he now felt the advancement of Age. But I was young, so he unleashed upon me his Intellect, his old Obsessions. We became teacher and pupil. I did not resist.

Oru new work was to exhume the ruined Cave, to retrieve the fragments of his ruin. Each day we laboured. Our first goal was to recover, intact, Crusoe's chest of Gold. Whereupon, I was paid wages in Gold, first at the apprentice and then at a journeyman rate. In the end, all Gold was mine, and Crusoe paid without Remorse.

Of my Education, always after working hours, first came Language. I pretended to know not one word of English; therefore, Crusoe "taught" me first these words: *Father, Son, Sin, Hell, Good Works, Salvation, Apocalypse.* Crusoe was amazed that I spoke English fluently—and so soon. To teach me to read, Crusoe wrote first letters, then words, and then his memory of Biblical passages on the sand of the beach. Soon, I could write a fair hand, could do sums quickly.

Being austere, Crusoe rejected my Convenience of moss-covered tree forks laved with honey; because of his example, I too came to find this practice boring, and yet my Sexuality did not wane. Therefore, one night during the incessant Spring rains, deep in our palmy, frond-lined Cave, I lay down beside Crusoe. I placed my head upon his chest—and he stiffened where he *lay*. Then my lips played lower along his Body until my breath pastured across his belly—and more. Yes, and more.

Oh, at first that thing between us was rude. Artfully, however, I showed Crusoe other more exotick things not learned by a common sailor, even on his longest Voyage. In the end, well-pleased, Crusoe accepted our Life for what it was.

In the end, I worked no more. Instead, I played all day, made kites, caused feathers to float long distances on the afternoon breeze, slept much in warm, curved stones on the beach—for such was my Nature.

This Indolence also came to an end, not by the return of black Savages, but by a white speck on the horizon. The speck became a topsail schooner, flying the colours of His Britannic Majesty: *The Huntress* out of Bristol under Captain Alexander Selkirk.

"What," Robinson Crusoe said, when the first boats landed to take on water. "What, sirs, is this year?"

"Why it's the year 1716. And why do you ask?"

With the water aboard, with my intention privately (and I felt almost passionately) affirmed by Captain Selkirk, with a chest of Gold now rightly mine, I deceived Crusoe.

At the time, of course, I knew he would have had it no other way.

In the dead of Night, before the first rays of the Sun, I rowed me in a small boat, and quietly boarded *The Huntress*. Because I had Gold—and for other more personal Reasons—I shared the Captain's quarters. We sailed for England with the tide.

Yes, Crusoe remained alone on his Island; and if alive is there to this day—for such was his nature. The choice was rational; almost certainly he wished it so. In all Candour, however, if I ever think of Crusoe, it is without Affection.

My desk lamp burns low. The first dark noises of another Winter rumble like carriage wheels through the streets of London.

My Flute & Cobbler is snug—and paid-for with Gold. My accounts are to-date.

This other Island, this England, is now my home; this Publik House is now my castle.

And who shall say I did not thus escape Crusoe's terrible dreams of Empire?

THREE POEMS

BORISLAV RADOVIĆ

Translated from the Serbo-Croatian by Aleksandar Nejgebauer

A SPECIAL PLACE

Shatter all evidence, raze every post
Covered with ashes, sunk in faded grass.
When you deny her, when you call her yours,
You love her, even while you insult her most.

She *is* your own,
This country,
The ancient rites, the long lewd carnivals:

Stretched out before your head, now turned.

She calls you. Here the myth comes to an end.

No longer can you stand there, looking on.
Close the broken window, the wrecked door behind,

Go, take your whole self, yield to her, all gone.

THE HEALING OF TIME

The air smells of snow, the earth of beer,
murky leaves stick to the creaking wheel.
Hear the warriors return to their wives.

With their helmets, memory too is removed,
the gray hair of stutterers uncovered.

Poets have little choice then: they speak
striving to bring out the poverty,
property and incestuous relations,
tracing the origins of young nations.

When toothless old women have washed their feet
ungirt, the warriors approach the cradles,
wondering at the white-headed infants.

Winter's the right time to establish paternity,
by the fire, when the one made to speak
is a man born blind,
his right arm crippled since childhood,
with the gift of healing time with idleness.

MILK AND HONEY

If only we knew, you and I,
whose house this is in the woods,
we would come to the threshold, searching
for the hollow where honey is found,
for the udder from which milk would flow;
we would spend our nights there, brow to brow:
two twin kernels inside their stone.

If only we could sit, you and I,
at the table in the house, at nightfall
we would listen to time squealing,
wandering through the cellar on tiny feet,
while between you and me
—like between palate and tongue—
milk and honey, our diet,
poured communion into earthenware vessels,
brightness of being into the speech of eyes.

MOURNING CRAZY HORSE

HAROLD JAFFE

5, September, 1877. Crazy Horse gone. Shoshone, Oglala, Lakota, Brulé.

I stand on the canyon floor in northeast Arizona looking up at the Anasazi petroglyph on the cliff wall: a humpbacked shaman dancing, playing a wooden flute. From Arizona I mean to head north.

When Dull Knife came with his starving Shyelas, Crazy Horse saw how it was. He left camp and went into the hills where squatting in the cold he fasted and dreamed. It was in a dream when he was a boy that he had seen his pony dance and had received his name. That was not so long ago, but it was a different time.

In Black Hat, New Mexico I stop for a drink in the only air-conditioned bar on the strip, the Holiday Inn. A young white man sitting next to me on his leatherette stool says that his name is Duane and begins to talk. He's out of work, nearly out of money, he's planning on going to Albuquerque to join a friend who bought a share in a Texaco service station franchise, he thinks he can get work there; "I'd better," he says, "if I don't, I don't know . . ." As he talks I hear the electronic whine and click and whistle of a pinball machine in the corridor. When I came in I noticed two boys five or six years younger than Duane at the machine. The waitress who delivers my beer in a frosted mug is trussed up in a kind of bunny costume, her thirtyish face tired and resigned, flaccid buttocks jiggling as she transports my dollar-fifty to the cash register. Beyond the murmur of the bar and pinball I can hear the eighteen-wheel semis revving up outside near the truckstop diner.

Crazy Horse's skin was oddly white for a Sioux. Or so it was said. He never permitted his "shadow to be caught" in a photograph. In Black Elk's account, Crazy Horse was thirty years old when he was murdered. Betrayed by Little Big Man. Crazy Horse's mother and father fastened up a pony drag and carried away their son's corpse (some said it was his heart which they had cut away from the corpse). None of the mourners followed them. It is said that they buried Crazy Horse in Wounded Knee Creek.

The neo sign atop the motel read: U TIRED
                                    HAVE REST
                                    KLIN UNITS
This is just south of Mt. Zion National Park in southern Utah. My room contains a color TV but only a 25-watt bulb in the reading lamp by the bed. The family in the adjoining "unit" keeps their tape recorder going in their pickup as they unload their luggage. I hear a country and western tune called "Lonesome, Ornery and Mean" by a male vocalist and two or three other tunes by a female with an affected vibrato. I lie on my back on the narrow bed and leaf through a magazine I picked up at a truckstop diner on the freeway . . .

The "Agency" wanted the Black Hills and finally they got what they wanted. They didn't want the Black Hills until the yellow metal that drives whiteskins crazy was discovered there. Then they wanted the hills very bad, and after many battles and other kinds of persuasion that they are expert at, they managed to get three or four chiefs to scratch their signatures on a long sheet of paper . . . After the Agency took the Black Hills Crazy Horse's dreams became deeper and longer-lasting than before. And the more immersed Crazy Horse became in his dreaming the more he gave away: bridle, headdress, blanket . . . Gifts to his people.

Called *Highway Evangelist,* the magazine contains millenarian quotations from the New Testament, as well as letters from readers, including this one:

Dear *Highway Evangelist,*

Have read a couple of yr issues and enjoyed them. Must tell you I love all those 18 wheelers. They fascinate me. If I was abt 25 yrs younger, wd sure like to drive one. But at 61, that's a little too old for that. So my wish now is to ride in one. Also wd like to make a collection of photos of 18 wheelers and drivers for a short history of each one. I sit at my window in the evenings and watch those big rigs go by. I know lots of the drivers from the Dakotas as I get to talk to them on my CB.

In town we have a diner where they stop to eat. I get to meet them and talk to them and some I know by name. It's real interesting listening to them. These men are a very special breed. Christ has to be with them. I say a little prayer for them all.

A nice trucker helped me one day when I had a blowout on I-90. He was from PA. Ever since we have been good CB buddies. He comes up to Fargo abt once a month. My CB handle is Indian Lady.

Thanks for letting me bend yr ear. If any trucker wd like to send me a photo of himself and his rig, wd love to have them.

Christ bless them all.

Hilde Wolcott
Box 352
Fargo, N.D. 04421

The available data, most of which are derived from oral sources, confirm that Crazy Horse was unsurpassed both as warrior and dreamer, that he was as unfailingly generous to his people as he was implacable to their oppressor. He was slight of build, with faded skin, and no one was considered stranger, more impenetrable. But his was the strangeness of genius, of sanctity. Or so the records indicate. His single child, a daughter, born to his wife Black Shawl, he named They Are Afraid of Her. She died before her fifth year of the choking cough transmitted by the white trader's sons. Crazy

Horse was murdered in his thirtieth year, in the Moon When the Calf Grows Hair.

After passing through Shining Mountain and over Mad River I find myself in a "family restaurant" in Orem, Utah, ordering the overpriced "special." Into my skull leaps the wild sentence I read in one of the Mormon pamphlets left in my motel room the evening before: "One year ago I received the gift of cancer."

Crazy Horse could not read, knew nothing of "world affairs," refused to be photographed, wore the "ghost shirt" but would not dance as the others did. When he led his braves into battle against the bluecoats he had them fight to kill and not to "count coups" or take trophy scalps.

Avoiding the "reservations," I drove from Oklahoma to Texas to New Mexico to Arizona to Nevada to Utah to Idaho to Montana to North Dakota . . . Aside from the sixteen-year-old Navaho boy who acted as my guide in Canyon de Chelly National Monument in northeastern Arizona, the only two other Indians I saw were in Las Rosas, New Mexico, and Clinton, Oklahoma, both drunk, one slumped on his spine against a railroad trestle, the other staggering back and forth on the strip asking for handouts. Possibly one other: a languid, pretty-faced adolescent in a truckstop diner near Amarillo. He was dressed like a cowboy, his white Stetson tipped back on his thick purple hair, an indolent dreamy look in his black eyes as he played one cowboy ballad after another on the jukebox.

When the warriors braided their ponies' tails and then painted their faces for war, the women made the tremolo in their rejoicing that their men would be killing the enemy. The braves meanwhile gave up their passion for their women, it being best that a warrior unsex himself, that he carry his grievance like a cold weight in his stomach. The sacred stone which Crazy Horse carried and which grew heavy in times of danger, had grown so heavy that his pony gave out. Worm gave Crazy Horse his own pony, a buckskin mare, her tail braided for war. This was before the battle in the valley of Rosebud where Crazy Horse led his braves to a victory over Three Star Crook and his column of bluecoats.

I exit the freeway at Rosebud, Montana. One of the guidebooks mentioned the Rosebud Museum. On the strip the Exxon attendant's deadpan creases into a vague glimmer of recognition after half a minute. "Take a right past the railroad tracks, follow the tracks for about a mile, mile and a half. You can't miss it."

Shoshone, Oglala, Lakota, Brulé.

I walk past the weeping birches and horse-chestnut trees up the stone steps into the cavernous Greek Revival structure. The difficult to define but unmistakable odor of chronic, senseless busy-work informs me that I am in the wrong place. I ask a janitor who points across the green to a narrow quonset hutlike building . . . A blonde young woman raises her head as I enter. The Rosebud Museum contains memorabilia from the years of the first white settlement to the present: photos and menus belonging to a gaggle of wives called themselves the "Rosebud Cowbelles," old saddles and water mills and prairie schooner fixtures, several photos of the Rosebud Little League baseball team, whose uniforms were "donated" by the Rosebud chapter of the VFW . . . The young blonde, in tight faded jeans and a brief cotton top, leads me around, managing often to bend, her tiny convex navel exposed like a pink peculiar genital, as she presses against this or that dusty display case.

Moon of the Dark Red Calf, 1877. Crazy Horse was spending most of his time dreaming and lamenting in the hills above the camp. It was said that he had unbraided his pony's tail and was through with fighting. But when his warriors showed their sadness, he joked with them, told them that the fighting was far from over. But it was bad. We all knew that it was bad.

In Medora, North Dakota, I drive into Theodore Roosevelt National Park, 70,000 acres of "badlands." Roosevelt hunted and ranched in these badlands in the 1880s and "fell in love with the plateaus and buttes and conical hills, with the many weird and brilliantly colored formations." When he took up residence in Washington he donated his ranchland to the national weal; this in effect was the beginning of our national park system. And this park "pays tribute to the contributions made by Teddy Roosevelt toward the conservation of our country's natural resources." So the plaque in the visitor center explains. I purchase a field guide to local flora, pay the park ranger at the desk, get into my car, turn around, and drive back out onto the freeway.

In the spring of 1877 Crazy Horse was told that the Great Father wanted him and the other big chiefs of the Sioux nation to travel to Washington to confer with him. This was in the Moon of the Grass Appearing. Crazy Horse declined to go. Also at about this time Crazy Horse learned that Three Star Crook was bribing Sioux warriors to help him fight the Nez Percés who were still holding out against the bluecoats in the northwest. It pained Crazy Horse to hear this, and he spoke out strongly against it in the sweat lodges, at the ghost dance gatherings, wherever he had access to the chiefs and elders.

Autumn, 1980. Our sweetest outlaws are bare chested, wear Stetsons, have a marketable patois, are reassuringly white-skinned, tattoo their rigs with Country, Playboy and Jesse James Christ, push their rigs to 80 on a downgrade, refuse to relinquish the passing lane on an upgrade, are the subjects of song, cinema, and beer commercials . . . The railroad, like a household Negro, shuffles from one dusty corner to another humming an old church tune.

Three Star Crook got wind of Crazy Horse's seditious counsels. He dispatched four companies of soldiers to "escort" Crazy Horse to Fort Robinson where, according to Three Star, the two of them would decide how best to remove the remaining Sioux to reservation land set aside for them near the Powder River. Crazy Horse, who had been fasting and dreaming for several consecutive days, had himself reluctantly concluded that the prospects of his people were at present without hope. After sending his braves away from camp into the hills, Crazy Horse awaited the soldiers.

Even on the freeway, driving east through Dakota, one feels the badlands, more implacable in their way than the Amazonian jungle, resisting (as the jungles have been unable to resist) "development."

They seep, these badlands, into the veins, like the residue of a crucial childhood dream, all unremembered but the texture, a fragment of texture . . . Coffee seeps. White-recorded history must not seep.

Once in Fort Robinson Crazy Horse was taken to a Major Lee, who while remaining seated behind his desk said only that it was now too late for talking. Instead Crazy Horse was placed under arrest and led away by two guards, one a whiteskin officer, the other Little Big Man. The same Little Big Man who had said many times that he would joyfully die fighting rather than turn the Black Hills over to the Agency was now himself an Agency policeman. Little Big Man actually spoke some words into Crazy Horse's ears, but they went unheard.

Still in the badlands, stopping at a "scenic overlook," I withdraw the field guide I bought in Roosevelt National Park and turn to a passage I underscored: "Certain of these species have a wild vitality, a kind of plant patience and persistence that has brought their kind through countless weather cycles and natural disasters. Most of them are profligate with seed . . . Some will lie dormant, awaiting a favorable season, for a century or even longer."

As they drew close to a wood and brick building Crazy Horse saw that the windows were barred with steel and that huddled within were braves, their legs and arms in irons. At once Crazy Horse lunged away, pulling a knife from his sash. But Little Big Man grabbed him from behind and while he held him that way a soldier bayoneted Crazy Horse in the stomach. The whiteskin soldier's name was William Gentles. It is not known whether Crazy Horse regained consciousness. He died that same night.

". . . at daybreak I roam,
ready to tear up the world
I roam . . ."

THE BERRY-PICKER

JAMES PURDY

JENSEN. Do they call you Donovan or Don . . . I know I asked you that question once before . . .

DONOVAN. Yes, several times . . .

JENSEN. Forgive me. (*Waits, then irritably.*) Well, which is it?

DONOVAN. Oh, excuse me, sir . . .

JENSEN. And you can dispense with the *sir*.

DONOVAN. Most people call me Donovan. Just a few say Don.

JENSEN. Then you prefer for me to call you Donovan too, I gather.

DONOVAN. That would be fine.

JENSEN (*putting on his glasses and looking at a paper*). You've been with me now just a week, but it seems longer somehow.

DONOVAN. I hope that doesn't mean the time has dragged, sir.

JENSEN. I didn't say it had, did I . . . Since my accident time and everything else has certainly changed. I mean my feeling about it. When I was with the team, there wasn't any time. I never had a minute to myself. Training, traveling, staying up all night with the fellows . . . (*Sensing he might be boring Donovan*) But I've told you all that before.

DONOVAN. There's one thing I fear I may have misrepresented about myself to you, sir, when we had that first interview . . . About my qualifications.

JENSEN (*both patiently and yet angrily*). Donovan, the *sir* has slipped out again. You watch that.

DONOVAN. It's because I respect you so much, you see . . . You were a kind of idol of mine. I felt you were the greatest hockey star of all . . . So, the *sir* sort of slips out . . . It doesn't mean I think you're old . . .

JENSEN. Or laid up on the shelf.

DONOVAN. You'll never be that . . . To me anyhow.

JENSEN. And what about the others.

DONOVAN. I think the others who loved you . . . I mean, respected and admired you . . . (*He becomes flustered.*)

JENSEN. We still get a lot of fan letters, that's for certain . . . But Donovan, you were saying that you had misrepresented yourself during the interview we had . . . When was that? (*As if to himself.*) Some two weeks ago only. (*He takes off his glasses.*)

DONOVAN. You asked me at that time if I was good at telling stories . . . Mr. Jensen, you know I have very little education . . . I told you the truth about that . . . But when I said I knew lots of stories, well that sort of just slipped out . . . I don't know any stories . . .

JENSEN. I don't remember even asking you that . . . I guess I did, though . . . But I don't like to be called *mister* any more than *sir*. When you say that I feel I will . . . always be sitting here . . .

DONOVAN (*almost desperately*). What shall I call you then . . . ? (*Almost says* "sir")

JENSEN. Niels.

DONOVAN. Niels . . . All right. (*Laughs nervously*) You see I can't even believe I am standing here beside you let alone addressing you so familiarly . . . You should see my scrapbook full of your pictures . . .

JENSEN (*not having heard him*). If I was to command you, you know just as a game, like we play checkers together, if I was to command you, Donovan, to tell me stories . . . Understand? Don't start so . . . What would you tell me.

DONOVAN. I beg your pardon . . .

JENSEN. I mean, since you brought up the subject, what kind of stories would you tell me . . . Supposing that is I was the typical demanding overbearing employer who wanted his money's worth, that is, wanted the bargain kept that he hear stories.

DONOVAN (*laughs almost hysterically*). I'm afraid I would disappoint you, then . . . (*Forcing it out*), Niels.

JENSEN (*pleased he has heard his Christian name*). . . . All right . . . Do you know something, Don . . . You make me hungry to hear one of the stories you don't know how to tell. (*They both laugh together, Donovan nervously, Jensen somewhat menacingly.*) I suppose if you were to tell me, say, a story, it would have to be about yourself.

DONOVAN. God forbid, sir . . .

JENSEN. Why do you say that?

DONOVAN. I mean, nothing about myself would or could interest you . . . I come from a very humble background . . . I told you or wrote you that on the application.

JENSEN. I didn't read the application.

DONOVAN (*shocked*). You didn't, sir?

JENSEN (*angrily*). Donovan!

DONOVAN. I'm sorry . . .

JENSEN. I hired you because I liked you on sight.

DONOVAN. Thank you.

JENSEN. And had you never mentioned these fucking stories I would never have remembered we made a bargain.

DONOVAN. Oh, Mr. Jensen.

JENSEN. What now!

DONOVAN. I'm somewhat surprised to hear you use such language . . .

JENSEN. What language.

DONOVAN. You used a word I just wouldn't associate with a man of your character . . .

JENSEN (*surprised*). I'm surprised a young man like you would be offended by a . . . mere word.

DONOVAN. It's not the word so much . . . It's that it came from . . . you, you see.

JENSEN. I guess I will have to be on my good behavior then with you around.

DONOVAN. Not at all . . . (*Forcing out the name*), Niels.

JENSEN. I don't think you should call me anything at all, Donovan . . . It . . . hurts you to call me anything, I do believe it does . . . So don't call me anything then.

DONOVAN. It gradually will come naturally to me . . .

JENSEN (*bitterly*). I don't think anything will ever come naturally to me again . . . if you ask me . . .

DONOVAN. I don't like to hear you say that, Niels.

JENSEN (*moved by his caretaker*). Why not, Donovan.

DONOVAN. I want to see you . . . yourself again.

JENSEN. That won't be.

DONOVAN. Even if we follow the doctor's orders . . .

JENSEN. Oh you mean the exercises, and the rubbing, and the cold ice packs and the rest . . . He just threw those in, the doc did.

DONOVAN. But if we tried . . . hard.

JENSEN. (*Moved by the young man's zeal, he almost touches him.*) No way.

DONOVAN (*breaking the silence*). I'll try to think of some stories for you . . . I know checkers bores you.

JENSEN. Everything bores me! I'm not me, don't you see . . . I'm not me. (*He looks down at himself.*) I almost wish you . . . no, no!

DONOVAN. What, sir? . . . What, Niels.

JENSEN. Nothing, nothing . . . It would frighten and terrify you . . . I have to not forget what a good boy you are.

DONOVAN. What do you mean by that, Niels.

JENSEN. You are, you know . . . That's why I didn't have to read your application paper. Your face was your application, Donovan. You don't even know it, do you . . . You make up for a lot, believe you me.

DONOVAN (*bewildered, but pleased*). I will tell you a story, Niels, if you like.

JENSEN. Look here, Donovan . . . Come over here. (*He takes his hand in his.*) You don't have to do a f . . . (*Stops himself*) damned thing but be yourself . . . Just be here with me . . . You're a ray of sunlight. (*Donovan goes to the back of the stage, brings out a bouquet of flowers and hands them to Jensen.*) What's this for?

DONOVAN. The other day when the chauffeur took us out for our spin, you said something about the flowers on the corner market . . .

JENSEN (*incredulous, too incredulous to be pleased*). You must be the first person who ever gave me . . . flowers . . . (*Moved and angry he has showed he is moved.*) Put them in water . . .

DONOVAN (*disappointed*). You didn't want them!

JENSEN. Did I say that . . . Put them in water . . . Go ahead! (*Donovan goes to back of stage, dispiritedly puts the flowers in a vase too large for them, and then puts the vase with the flowers on a table some distance from Jensen.*) Donovan, I would like my medicine now.

DONOVAN. It's quarter of an hour shy of the time for it, Niels . . .

JENSEN. I can't wait.

DONOVAN. I don't understand . . .

JENSEN. It's hurting bad . . .

DONOVAN. But the doctor warned . . .

JENSEN. Do we have to obey him in everything?

DONOVAN. In medicine, I think so . . .

JENSEN. Come over here . . . Come on . . . (*He takes his hand.*) You're afraid of me! (*Throws down Donovan's hand, and pushes him away.*)

DONOVAN. I respect you too much, that's all.

JENSEN. You fucking liar! (*Donovan turns away in sorrow and confusion.*) You go over there and get that medicine . . . I can't take this nagging pain . . . Do you hear?

DONOVAN. Maybe if I rubbed it . . .

JENSEN. Yeah, maybe, if you have the guts that is to touch me there . . . If you don't respect me too much to put your hand on me . . .

DONOVAN. Niels, you are my all.

JENSEN (*amazed*). Did I hear you right.

DONOVAN. I think so . . . I'll get your medicine now . . . It's only ten minutes shy . . .

JENSEN (*to himself*). And what's ten minutes in hell, huh. (*He looks at the flowers longingly. Donovan has gone to the cabinet, has taken down the medicine and the tumbler of water, and now brings them to Jensen.*) Was I ever so glad to see anything as those two tiny little red pills. (*He takes them from Donovan's hand and then accepts the tumbler of water.*) Now all I have to do is wait, eh, Donnie? Just wait . . .

DONOVAN. Perhaps if I put my hand there, on the base of your spine you know, it would also give you some relief . . .

JENSEN. I think the pills will do the trick . . . Unless of course . . . you want to . . . (*Angry*) It's up to you.

DONOVAN. The doctor ordered gentle massage there . . .

JENSEN. If I did all he ordered, I'd be sick for ten thousand years. (*Donovan has been moving slowly toward him, he loosens Jensen's bathrobe and gently touches the base of his spine in a few movements. Suddenly:*) That'll be enough . . . Quit! Do you hear . . . Stop . . . (*Donovan moves slowly away from Jensen. Jensen suddenly breaks down, sobbing, puts his head in his hands weeping deliriously.*) I can't stand it . . . I want to die . . . If you want to give me presents, why the fuck don't you kill me . . . Nobody would blame you! (*Weeps deliriously*)

DONOVAN (*terrified, helpless*). Niels . . . Niels . . . (*Drawing near him in spite of his fear*) Niels.

JENSEN. Why don't you call me *sir*, and shame me some more . . . Go ahead, call me *sir*. Go on.

DONOVAN. Niels. The pills will help soon. (*He takes his hand.*)

JENSEN (*suddenly raising his head, takes Donovan's head in his two hands, kisses him*). Does that make you sick to your stomach.

DONOVAN. You know better, I think . . .

JENSEN. Why don't you tell me one of your stories you are always promising me . . . And bring those flowers over closer, why don't you . . . On account of nobody ever brung me flowers . . . Not even in the hospital when they took my spine out and put it back again . . . Well, what story have you elected to tell me . . .

DONOVAN. Oh, Niels . . .

JENSEN. On account of we don't like checkers, we don't like rides in our Cadillac no more . . . And we got tired of banana splits and strawberry parfaits, at least I did . . .

DONOVAN. The only story I can seem to remember is when I was a young boy . . .

JENSEN. Well, that ain't too long ago then . . .

DONOVAN. It seems . . . long . . .

JENSEN. As long as when you came to care for me?

DONOVAN. A different long ago, yes.

JENSEN. Donovan, take my hand . . . Just until the pain quits.

DONOVAN. Is it easing, do you think.

JENSEN. If you take my hand . . .

DONOVAN (*puts his hand in Jensen's, but it is clear he is thinking of his "story." He begins*). It was a soft summer day not too different from now, except we lived in the country, my mother and my three brothers and I . . .

JENSEN. Where was this?

DONOVAN. In Maine . . . *My mother said, "You know what would please your two older brothers who are working hard in the fields today with the new haymowing machine they bought in town . . . If you was to go up in the mountains and gather some fresh blueberries I would make us some blueberry muffins for supper." "I'll go," I told my mother . . . "I will indeed . . ." I went up the tallest mountain and got enough berries I think to make muffins for threshers . . . Then just as I was about to come down the mountain and go home, for it was getting later than I thought . . . I saw this house with a thin line of smoke curling out the chimney . . . I stepped into the yard, then I heard someone singing, I walked up the steps to the front door, I heard a woman say, "Come in, Johnny, come in . . ." I walked over to the door, and there was a woman who looked almost like my mother, only she was I think prettier and younger, except there was no one prettier or younger than my mother . . . "You're just in time, Donnie," she said, though it sounded like Johnny too when she said it, which was what she called me when she had kept me home sick from school . . . "You've brought me the berries, haven't you," she said . . . "Yes," I replied, "but where are Otis and Maurice . . . ?" "They're not back from haying yet, but we won't wait, dearest, for it's getting so late and I wanted to have this bowl of berries just with you . . . We can bake the muffins later . . . I wanted this little repast by ourselves . . . See, the fresh cream I just got from the cow, did you ever!" We sat down and ate the berries . . . They were the sweetest fruit I ever ate . . . And the cream . . . Never before or after did I taste its equal . . . But suddenly I felt so very tired, a climb up that mountain you know and the visit to the strange house, and Mama, looking herself and yet far younger . . . Then I came out of my drowse and was alone . . . But there sat the two empty bowls with the stain of berries and fresh cream . . . I ran then for night was coming, and it threatened rain . . . I ran down the mountain and to our house, picking enough berries on the way to make some muffins . . . I heard a church bell ringing in the distance . . . There were a few drops of rain already from the northwest . . . There was a knot of people I could see gathered on Mama's front steps as I approached the house . . . My two brothers, still in their work clothes, came down the steps and took me by*

*the hand, and held me tight . . . They said, "Our dear mother,
Donovan, our dear mother is dead . . ."* (*Waits*) That's my story
. . . Did you listen?

JENSEN. Did I listen! Did I listen.

DONOVAN. Did you like my story?

JENSEN. Do you know any more like it.

DONOVAN. I thought I told you, it was my only story.

JENSEN. Thank God for that.

DONOVAN. You didn't like, then, my storytelling.

JENSEN. Like it! Are you supposed to like a story like that . . .
Good God . . .

DONOVAN. Well I won't ever burden you with another . . . Is
your pain gone . . .

JENSEN. One pain is gone, and another took its place . . .

DONOVAN. I'm sorry I don't tell the stories you're used to . . .

JENSEN. What do you mean, *I'm used to* . . . Nobody ever told
me a story before, and I don't think anybody will ever tell me one
like it afterward.

DONOVAN. If you would like me to rub the sore spot . . .

JENSEN. I got a sore spot no human hand can ever reach to . . .

DONOVAN. You didn't like the story I told you.

JENSEN. I liked it too much, that's the truth . . .

DONOVAN. You did . . .

JENSEN. It busted me . . . I won't never be the same . . . I
don't see you the same. What do you mean I didn't like it. Don't
you see what it done to me . . . Don't you see?

DONOVAN. It's got so dark in the room I can't . . .

JENSEN. Come over closer, sit down . . . I wish you wouldn't
act as though I was going to eat you alive, Donovan . . . Oh Dono-
van . . . Donovan . . . What's to fear in a wreck like me, don't
you know that . . . I couldn't touch a fly now . . .

DONOVAN. Niels, you were the greatest, the best . . .

JENSEN. Who cares about *were* or *was.*

DONOVAN. I do.

JENSEN. You do.

DONOVAN. You bet.

JENSEN. You care a lot.

DONOVAN. I think I do . . .

JENSEN. And you won't run out on me like the others . . . You won't leave me like your mother left you . . .

DONOVAN. She was called, Niels . . . She didn't want to leave me . . . She was called.

JENSEN. Don't ever tell me another story that beautiful, Donovan . . . If you want me to stay among the living . . .

DONOVAN. I won't leave you. I thought you knew that from the beginning . . .

JENSEN. I hoped it . . . But what is hope in this life . . .

DONOVAN. It's something . . .

(*Jensen draws him close to him against his breast.*)

THE RIVER

JAMES LAUGHLIN

ABOUT "THE RIVER"

"The River" was written in 1935 in Paris. In my freshman year at Harvard I had won the Story *magazine short story contest, and I convinced the dean that if I could have a leave of absence to wander around Europe I would become a famous writer such as Hemingway and Fitzgerald. It didn't work out that way, but I have no regrets about getting to know Europe.*

I had hardly any money for the trip—my parents thought it was a frivolous expedition—but happily there was dear Cousin Anne, who "understood." She sent me a few dollars every month, and in those days of the favorable exchange a few dollars went a long way. In Paris I found a tiny room at the back of an insurance agency near the Champ de Mars which cost seven dollars a month, and I took my meals at workingmen's restaurants.

It was a rather lonely life as I had no friends my own age. The "Craig" of the story was entirely fictional (perhaps my doppelgänger?) My best friend was the incomparable Gertrude Stein. Her influence is present everywhere in the style of the story. I came to know Miss Stein entirely by chance. In the schwimmbad at Salzburg I met her best French friend, Bernard Fay, the Sorbonne professor of Franco-American history. He took me with him to Gertrude's beauiful farm near Belley in the Savoie, and I was able to stay a month as she found work for me.

That fall Miss Stein was going to the States for her American lecture tour, and her agent had told her she must have one-page summaries of each lecture to give the reporters. Boiling down twenty pages of very cerebral Steinese into simple journalese was as difficult as anything I've ever attempted—some pieces had to be done five or six times to satisfy her—but in the end the work was accomplished. Alas, I have lost my copies of these masterpieces.

My other task was to change tires. Every afternoon Miss Stein and Alice B. Toklas would set out for a ride in their little Ford. They sat in the front, and I sat in the back with two horrible dogs who spent their time trying to lick me, Basket, a white poodle, and Pepe, a little Mexican yipper. There were many punctures every day. I would change the tires while the ladies sat in the grass admiring the view. But Miss Toklas's cooking made up for everything.

I did not do much actual writing when I got back to Paris. Mostly I thought about the great things I was going to write while I wandered the streets of the city. My favorite walks were along the banks of the Seine. I would browse in the bookstalls, looking at the books I could not afford to buy, or sit on the stone parapets watching the life on the river. In a way the flow of the Seine became the movement of my life, going somewhere, but where?

When I returned to Harvard and started New Directions, "The River" was the third in a little series of pamphlets I brought out (in 1938). Why reprint it now? Sentimentality and nostalgia, I suppose: an attempt to recapture the lost past.—J. L.

You can go on moving around, thinking it's the place and not you, for a good while, trying the mountains and this city and that, even trying English country, which is about as far as an American can go, and then finally after you've spent most of your money and worn out two or three typewriter ribbons without getting anything done, you begin to see and know that it's not the places it's just you. Then if you have any sense you go back to Springfield and teach school or try to get a job in the bank and pretty soon the outlying cousins are saying how that crazy Carson is settling down and maybe'll come to something after all.

Craig and I wouldn't have come to be saying we didn't have

·sense, but when we got to Paris along about August, knowing then it wasn't the fault of the places where we'd been, we knew we ought to give up and go home, but we knew even more we'd rather do anything else. And so, as Craig said, rather than go home and start brawling with our families again, we would just sit still in Paris watching the sun shine and the Seine flow, hoping it wouldn't rain more than two days a week. We did and it didn't. In fact it was about the best weather we'd had anywhere, good and hot so you knew it was summer all right but none of those stinkers that you get in Wisconsin and hardly any rain.

The Seine was dirty, so dirty we didn't dare try swimming in it for fear of catching something, but it did flow in a quiet steady way that made me feel at home. (I've never liked New York because the river isn't in the middle of it where it ought to be. For me it has always been that a city that is a city is a city built on two sides of a river with each side about equal in importance. And Paris is like that. There are more of what the tourist maps call monuments on the right bank, but on the left bank you see twice as many people who look good for something, which keeps the two sides balanced. Then there is Notre Dame in the middle being a fulcrum, that is, at least, as far as I'm concerned it's a fulcrum.)

In Salzburg, where we had been in July, we had gotten used to a rushing roaring river, a river fairly blowing it's head off to get wherever it's going. Wherever we went in Salzburg, even when we were stymied by one of those little bergs that crop up like pimples all around the town, we could feel the Salzach plunging along, almost jumping out of its bed. It was an excited river, and we were excited too, excited by being face to face with our futures, really alone with our future lives for the first time. The Salzach was an excited river. One day as we were crossing it Craig described the Salzach perfectly: he looked down from the bridge at it and said, "Yessir, she'll be comin' round the mountain when she comes!"

So the Seine seemed quiet to us when we first got to Paris, quiet and a little contemptible. (You'll wonder why we even noticed the river in a big busy city like Paris, but I'll tell you that water is such a thing to me that wherever I am it is the thing I see first last and longest.) But soon we were liking it better, soon liking it very well as we walked slowly along the quais in the late evening as the lights came on, and soon we were knowing that its slow steady flowing pleased us perfectly. Our time came to be the Seine's time, and again and again I stopped when crossing a bridge to lean over the wall and watch for a long time the brown water moving and yet staying, speaking but silent, hurrying yet delaying.

In Salzburg our living had been like the river there, intense and driven. We thought then we were going somewhere and wanted to hurry. We were pushed and pulled, pushed by the memory of what life had been like at home and pulled by the desire for success which would give us permanent escape. There was really nothing exceptional about our life at home (we lived in Springfield, Wisconsin); we were more or less typical—sensitive boys wanting to live a life of books and feeling smothered by the indifference of the people around us to the things we idolized. Springfield had a library, one of those Carnegie libraries that you find in small cities, but it had no books in it by Proust or James Joyce or Ezra Pound. Springfield had occasional concerts, but the pianists never played anything but Chopin and the singers sang "On the Road to Mandalay." There was an art shop in Springfield—it sold reproductions of "The Last Indian." There were pretty girls in Springfield but most of them thought Craig and I were flits and made us miserable; not one of them could have stood still or kept quiet for three minutes. How did we know about things like that? A teacher in the high school, a young English teacher. He was different. He came from the East. He understood. And Craig and I had become his intimates, draining from him his store of good things from the other world for which we came to long. We were with him constantly. He was a poet. And we were poets. We dreamed together—he was only seven years older than Craig and I—of life in Paris, of life in the hill towns, of a better, richer life far, far away from Springfield. Yet there was nothing exceptional in this; there are boys dreaming such dreams in every city in America. The exceptional thing was that we were able to try to live them, able to get away from the home we so despised while we were still young enough really to despise it.

It came about through Craig's grandmother. She persuaded our families to let us go. She understood us too. She could not understand the books we read or the things we talked about but she could understand what was happening inside us and put some sort of true value on it. Our parents could understand it in a way—we were not the first boys in Springfield to get ideas. But to them our leanings were just a phase, something annoying, like the measles, through which we safely would pass in time, to be in the end like them. Oh they *understood* us well enough! They were decent as could be. They let us have money for books and did not mind our being continually with Charles Herrick, but they were never for us. They never really thought it would be a wonderful thing if one of us should turn out to be a famous writer, or that it would be a better thing than our turning out to be moneymaking business men. But Craig's grandmother did understand us. She had never known a poet in her life but she could think of our being such a thing without feeling self-conscious about it. She was a larger mind than the rest, not a more developed mind, but one larger to begin with, capable of a wider natural knowledge. She was not dissatisfied with life in Springfield but she could realize that there were other places in the world where life could be as good and even better perhaps. That our parents could not do. Their imagination did not go beyond having the best house in Springfield. They might have filled it with expensive paintings from Italy if they had made that much money—they were not hicks, they made trips to New York and to California—they simply never thought of life anywhere else being possibly life for them. I imagine that they would really have rejected France because it had no bathtubs.

But Craig's grandmother got around them. She liked us. Without herself being in any way a rebel she could appreciate rebellion. She could sense that a distaste for life in Springfield might not be a weakness in our characters. She liked us. We often brought Herrick to her house and overwhelmed her with our immensities of superior wisdom. It was all Greek to her—she was not bookish—but she liked it. And she persuaded our families to let us go when we'd been graduated from high school. She persuaded them by saying it would be the quickest way to get us over it, to let us go and rub our noses in it. "They'll come back after a year and go to college and that will be the end of it," she told our parents. But those were not her real feelings, that was just her craft, a craft in which she was being perfectly honorable because she felt it was for our good. She didn't think we would get over it. She hoped we wouldn't. She wanted more for us than success in Springfield.

I think though that what probably finally decided Craig's father and mine (they were close friends) to let us go was the idea of showing Springfield that they were well enough off to give us trips abroad before we began college. I think the phrase "grand tour" and something of its connotation had permeated into Springfield.

And so we went. We were in the odd class that finished high school in February and we crossed over in March. And August found us in Salzburg, full of excitement, and confident of the wonders ahead of us. We weren't ridiculous. We had a sense of humor, if it was a little undeveloped. We didn't think that one glimpse of an oxcart would turn us into geniuses, but we were sure that things would be different in Europe, that the barriers inside us that had kept us from writing anything more startling at home than fairly adept imitations would somehow be moved away by the new life. In America we had known that what held us back was the atmosphere and not something in ourselves.

And we still thought so in Salzburg, in spite of the barren weeks in Munich (nice old atmosphere and lots of culture but not too much diversion), the Dolomites (what we need are the primitive realities—rocks and peasants), Ragusa (get out of this damn rain, get the sun, life force), Vienna (blend of Teutonic and Celtic spirits, just the thing), and Budapest (need more color). We still didn't realize that the only thing that stimulated us was finding good excuses to disturb the travail of composition. Craig had gotten around to justifying his obscurity (somehow his lines didn't seem to have much "style" when they had also to make sense) by saying that psychoanalysis had driven poetry to associational logic, and I had actually reached chapter XI in my autobiographical novel, although somehow my scene had managed to get itself shifted from Springfield to the more exotic quarters of Vienna. As I say, in Salzburg, with the Salzach running itself ragged beside us and inside us, we were still energetically stubbing our toes on our own heels.

And then we had seventeen hours in a smelly third-class carriage to Paris with plenty of time to think and no mask of atmosphere or ritual between ourselves and the mirror. We didn't talk about it at all, we didn't even discuss what we'd do in Paris, but when we got there we both knew, though we didn't admit it at first, that it wasn't the fault of the places we'd been but just ourselves. All day we sat watching the rain-soaked country go by, watching the rain fall steadily against the gloomy station walls where the train stopped, while more and more the forced confidence of our early-morning start faded into uncertainty and doubt melted into despair. And after night came, hiding the rain and locking us tightly into our stale-smelling wooden box, there wasn't the least struggle left in us, in either of us; we were done for and we knew it and we didn't care enough anymore to mind.

So, soon the Seine seemed fine to us, as we were going no faster than it was, hardly moving at all, just letting ourselves be washed pleasantly along. At first we stayed at a fairly good hotel on the Quai Voltaire (the one where they say that an American lady saw a gendarme under her bed and moved right on to Berlin without saying a word) but that was too expensive and we moved to the Pretty Hotel in the Rue Amalie back near the Champ de Mars. It was an awful quarter to live in, not tough or dirty but just messy and sloppy, but the room was big and cheap and after all, as Craig said, if you couldn't afford the St. James et d'Albany the next most distinguished certainly was the Pretty. We were there almost a week before we caught on to the nature of the Pretty's principal business, though two or three nights the banging around on the stairs had woken us up, and not having our own bathroom we thought we would be better off the quicker we ditched the Pretty, which we did.

Walking down the Rue Saint-Dominique one day we'd seen a Chambres-à-Louer sign hanging out a window and we went there. It was an insurance agent who had his office on the second floor of an old apartment house; he had the whole floor and there were some little rooms in the back that he didn't use. We got two for less than we had been paying for one at the Pretty, which suited me fine because, much as I like Craig, I'd gotten tired of looking at his dirty shirts lying around in corners, and besides I have always hated to be looked at by anyone while I'm busy waking up in the morning. We almost moved again after a few days when we found out that one of the rooms down the hall belonged to a great big black man, but we finally decided that, as Craig said, miscegenation was better than moving again. So we stayed, and then in a few weeks we were calling the black man Sambo and buying him drinks at the corner bistro while he told us about the war and all the French women he'd had in a mixture of broken-down French and even worse English that he'd picked up from an English spinster in Arles who had paid him well, he said, for just coming to sit with her of an evening. After getting out of the army, Sambo had managed to marry a solid widow who politely had died at once leaving him enough to enjoy Paris for a few years before going home to his brother Sengalese.

So we stayed and the quiet waiting ways of Paris grew into us. We found a little restaurant in the quarter where they would cook eggs for us at ten in the morning, we got used to coffee with chicory in it, we learned the bus routes and got caught riding first class in the Metro, we didn't bother anymore to get our pants pressed, we began picking up some argot, and we even got used to keeping the covers on our typewriters all day.

As I say, the weather in Paris that August was all you could have asked for, sun every day but never so hot that you sweated when you walked the way you do in August back at home. We walked a lot, usually in the evenings when the coming darkness seemed to stir a breeze, not going anywhere in particular, just strolling along the quiet streets and busy boulevards, talking a little now and then about the things we saw, the people we passed and the houses, the people walking quickly to get somewhere, the people walking slowly as were we, the people sitting on little chairs before their doors, talking and watching, the houses we passed, the houses some hard, some soft, sometimes like pictures but more often not, walking and sometimes talking, walking slowly, talking lightly, not hurrying and not delaying, hardly thinking what we were saying; so walking and so lightly quietly talking, we often saw and surely came to know the way the light dies and the night comes softly on.

And we sat.

We learned to like to sit and watch, to sit and sip, to sit and sit. For Paris is a sitting city.

There is no city anywhere that sits as Paris sits, that sits so much, so often, or so everywhere. And soon we were sitting and waiting, or sitting and worrying, as is the American way, but watching and gently talking. At first we sat when we were tired of walking and then we came to sit for sitting's sake. We sat a lot, in many places both by day and night.

We sat at big cafés on boulevards and at little ones on side streets. We sat on park benches sometimes and never on park chairs because we couldn't bear to pay the chairkeepers. In the mornings before lunch we would sit at one of the cafés near the Opera, reading the paper and our mail if we had any, our mail from home that we rushed each day to the American Express office to collect and then never liked when we read it. We never liked them, the half angry half loving letters from our families back in Springfield, but we would always read them, each reading his own first and then reading it to the other. They didn't bore us or make us homesick, they only made us vaguely uneasy, because we knew that the life they told about would always be more real to us than that we were living, much as we hated it and wanted to escape from it. And they made us think of our families as we didn't want to, made us neither hate them nor love them, but only realize how wholly we were bound to them, how surely we would never cease to be what they had made us. We read our letters and then as we sat watching people come and go, sipping a vermouth or perhaps a Pernod, made up in our minds elaborate answers to them which we finally never wrote.

And as we sat and watched we read the *Paris Herald* through, first skipping from page to page, then reading every word. It was a daily ritual, completely meaningless and very satisfying, to read it all, to read the whole dull paper which was exactly the same every day. We read all the *Paris Herald* every day and never anything else, easily forgetting all about the solid classics in pocket editions that we'd carted around Europe to feed our souls on. We read everything in that paper and liked it. Just watching the news of the world floating by on the front page seemed to give us a sense of action, to establish us against time, and never did the editor fill space by printing the whole passenger list of an incoming liner but we read every name, never recognizing that of anyone we knew, but somehow enjoying the certain knowledge that these were their names. We read all the personal items in the society column and tried to figure out which ones had been sent in by the people themselves. Naturally, we had no way of telling, but sometimes from the name we could be sure it was that of a person who liked to see himself in print. We read the stupid Republican editorials that someone told us were written by Englishmen. We read the financial articles which we didn't understand. We read the letters from pacifists, puzzlemakers, amateur politicians, and ladies exchanging recipes, and thought up sarcastic answers to them which we never sent in to the paper. We read, as I say, the whole paper and liked it, but most of all two things: Sparrow Robertson and the baseball games. Back at home we would never have read the sports page at all as a matter of principle, but there in Paris at the big cafés, sitting and sipping, watching and reading, we came to be liking that part best of all.

There is one good reason why the *Paris Chicago Tribune* could never really rival the *Paris New York Herald* and that is Sparrow Robertson. You have got to read him to believe him possible. I suppose Sparrow Robertson would call himself a philosopher of sport, but to me he will just always be the great living master of American prose. If I were to quote things he has written, you wouldn't see what I was talking about. No, you have got to come on Sparrow Robertson's literary pearls by yourself, to stumble on them yourself in the middle of his dignified account of the last boxing match at the Palais des Sports or a hailstorm of statistics about horseracing results in 1910. Now I wouldn't want to give a wrong impression and have you think that Sparrow Robertson ever gave way to unnecessary rhetoric or even sporting jargon, because he is, I assure you, a very serious artist indeed. No, it is only that sometimes his enthusiasm for expression, his great affection for his subject, leads Sparrow by the way of certain lapses of grammar, certain variants from the accepted order, which are so individual, or let us say, so quite apart, in fact so gorgeously and beautifully things unto themselves that there is I assure you nothing in the heavens nor on earth to measure the joy, the orgasmic abdominal joy, with which the reader thereof is instantaneously seized. For you see old pal Sparrow has a way of saying things that is really kinda funny.

But it was really the baseball that mattered most. As I remember that time it is this that I remember, the passionate way we felt about the Cardinals slowly catching up on the Giants. Now I couldn't even tell you who finally did win the pennant that year, in fact I think in the end it wasn't either the Cardinals or the Giants, but still there is something left in me of the way I was feeling about it then, the passionate death-and-destiny way I was feeling about the Cardinals slowly catching up with the Giants. There was no obvious reason for liking one team better than the other, but somehow the verbiage of the sportwriters who were playing up the race between them did its work on us, and we began to feel excited and concerned. Neither of us had ever been in St. Louis, but really the teams didn't mean places to us anyway. They didn't mean places or even ideas to us, it was their slow steady struggle, the tortured rising and falling of their percentages as they won and lost games, the gradual catching up, the sudden spurts ahead and falling back, the agony or joy of two games won or lost on the same day, the nervousness of games divided, the exciting certainty that the Cardinals would finally catch up mixed with the worrying doubt that their luck might change and they wouldn't, these were the things that were meaning so much to us then, this constant excitement of fighting against chance, assurance against doubt, ourselves and the Cardinals against the Giants and luck. It seems foolish that we should have cared at all, and yet even now, when suddenly something makes that time come back inside me, I can feel a little of the feeling that we had, the tense exciting feeling that we had.

So our morning sitting wasn't quiet, when we read the papers and the letters from home. But in the afternoons we had a very different kind of quiet pleasant sitting.

Then we went into little hidden streets, where at deserted bistros bad-tempered old women would serve us dirty glasses of stale beer that we could hardly swallow. In gray and dusty side streets we sat away our afternoons; watching the people come and go who don't walk for pleasure, watching the flow of life that does not see itself because its living is too close and real. Mornings and evenings we saw Gay Paree, but afternoons we saw Chelsea and the East Side, every shabby street from South Boston to Bucharest, empty of life and full of living, the quickslow fatlean oldyoung shabby ones who have no names. We sat and saw them endlessly ever and never the same, an endless broken-rhythmed movement from somewhere to somewhere and nowhere to nowhere. Each time we saw the kind of face or step or look we thought we knew, we knew the more we knew nothing. We thought we knew we were, and then we weren't so sure; we only knew this moving, this coming and going, slow steady flowing from nothing to nothing, from zero to infinity.

Dusty sunlight in a faded street.

"What does it mean, Craig, where are they going, where are we going?"

"You tell me, why don't you!"

Dusty sunlight and the noises far and near, city sounds that rise and fall and never die, a voice of many tones, speaking the words we hear but cannot understand.

"What can we do, Craig, to make it stop for a minute, to make the whole damn thing stop and look at us for a minute?"

"You're asking me?"

Dusty sunlight and the feeling of old stone and the feeling of blood, not the quick blood of a wound, but the slow, stale blood of life's endless seepage. "Look, Craig, look at that dog over there in the gutter; it's free! It doesn't see what we see! It doesn't have to try to understand!"

At night we sat at the big cafés in Montparnasse and tried not to look like Americans. "We can never do it," Craig used to say, "until we get suits with pointed lapels and stop wearing crêpe-soled shoes." We would have liked to do the boîtes on Montmartre, but we didn't have the money to waste; we had to go places where we could sit for a long time without spending much. So we sat at the Dôme and the Rotonde and wondered what they had been like in the good old days before all the Americans went home to Connecticut. There were still young Americans to be seen around in various states of intoxication, but they none of them looked as though they might be Hemingways or Harry Crosbys or McAlmons. Most of them looked as though they might be medical students or bank clerks, and certainly none appeared to be wearing the black hat very hard. We sat at the bright noisy corner and tried not to look like Americans, while we talked about nothing else except America, and why we were Americans and what it meant and what we were going to do about it. I don't remember what we said anymore; there was a lot of talk about time concepts and the sensuality of motion, about the abstraction of materialism and deracination, about lack of resistance by tradition and even the melting pot. There was endless talk about the American Scene and Pure Art, and of it all I remember almost nothing. It was serious and completely unimportant, and we forgot what we had said one night in time to say it again the next.

We sat and watched and knew that we were waiting for something to happen, as every American must wait for something to happen, and gradually grew more and more content to have what was to happen be nothing happening at all. Almost we ceased to care to think we knew what we were waiting for. We sat and watched.

Naturally, as you might expect, the great diversion of our evening sitting was that of watching the girls. Back home in Springfield we had always heard the usual stories about the women of Paris, and now that we were there seeing them, we could see that there was a reason for all the talk. As Craig said, having looked over the

Françaises he could understand why the frogs didn't want the Germans to get Paris. Sitting there at the Dôme and the Rotonde we saw some mighty interesting specimens, and seeing them we were wishing all the time that we were a lot richer and more experienced and less generally terrified of something that had been a continual source of speculation for years without ever ceasing to be a hopelessly insoluble problem. And so we watched and joked, savoring in imagination the thing we wanted but didn't dare to touch. It wasn't that both of us hadn't had the usual adolescent experiences, or that we didn't know, or think we knew, about all there was to the subject, but somehow there was an impassable barrier between the Springfield high school girls whom you pawed in rumble seats and the Paris poules who stared at you with unconcealed contempt. And so we sat and watched and wondered, yearning with mind and body, trying vainly to believe that we were being sensible and mature and only succeeding in feeling more intensely the frustration of our immaturity.

It's true that we did have one mild adventure, but that only served to increase our discontent, increasing desire without increasing confidence or removing doubt. It was nothing extraordinary—two obviously nonprofessional young females who gave us the eye one night as we were walking across the Champ de Mars and picked us up when they found we didn't have the savoir faire to do it ourselves. At this point Craig took control of the situation, attaching to himself the better looking of the two and leading the way down one of the more obscure and less public paths of the gardens that lie beneath the Eiffel Tower. I can't say that I had a particularly good time. The girl was too eager and I was clumsy with her, but at least I found that the difference in language was a great help. Trying to say something in situations where absolutely nothing was to be said had always given me an unnatural horror of them. But that night, having only to talk with lips and hands, above all knowing that I would never have to see the girl again, I had less separation of mind and body, less the feeling of being a ridiculous fool. But after my heat had risen and then cooled, when repeated caresses were no longer a crescendo that swept along the mind in the body's ascent, when kiss after kiss was like the banging of a bad chord, mere product of inertia, when nothing remained of the first excitement but a boredom half disgust; when I had suddenly left the girl without a word, pushed her away, risen, turned, and gone away in a single motion, walking as fast as I could without once looking back until I had come to the edge of the river; then, as I slowly went along the bank, watching the water moving in the spots of mirrored light, feeling the stillness of the silent river in the sleeping night, I felt again, as I had felt before, that these things I had done, the things that had been done to me, could never really have importance, could never be all to me that I wanted them to be, all that I had read and sensed that they could be, until the person for whom they were done and who did them was one speaking to more of me than the body alone. For all of its being in Paris this was no more to me than had been similar experiences in the country roads outside of Springfield. It increased my desires without giving me any greater reason for them.

But with Craig it was otherwise, for he told me next day, though I had done everything I could to keep him from bringing up the subject, that his girl had been a "pretty hot little number" and that she had "given him a real good workout considering it was free." And I could see that the thing had started up in him a new kind of inside movement that had not been there before, for from then on, though he didn't say it, I could see that the half unhappy pleasure of our quiet watching waiting life in summer Paris was no longer so much for him as it had been. He began to get restless and he didn't talk in the same way as he had been talking; I could see that there was a separation taking place inside him and that he was no longer content to be drifting without a good American goal to hold on to. I could see growing in him the need to be working toward something definite. I could feel the American in him coming back to rule him, could see him beginning to feel that time was wasted in which something wasn't done and that walking and talking, sitting and sipping, watching and waiting, were not enough to make a completed life. He didn't start to work again at his poetry, but he read again and seemed hardly to notice the quiet life around him but only to notice the busy moving life, to realize that time was going on without him. He was changing, as I say, and I could see it but I didn't say anything, because I knew that it would only make it go faster. I knew the change would be, but I was sorry for it.

Somehow I knew the day on which he would go, the boat on

which he would sail, before he even tried to break the news to me. And somehow he sensed from the way I answered him, that there was no need for him to explain anything, that I quite understood and that I would not try to change his mind. I didn't and he bought his ticket. We agreed that he would tell my parents that I had joined up with two English boys whom we had gotten to know in Paris who were "very steady and quite all right," so that they wouldn't think I was alone and try to make me come home, and that he would spread the word around in Springfield that I was putting the finishing touches on a novel that a big London publisher was just waiting to publish. Craig left me his American razor blades, and the night before he sailed we celebrated the end of our partnership with champagne, but as we could only afford a half-bottle, we neither of us managed to work up much gayety. I was sorry to see him go, but not as much as I should have expected if I'd known it was going to happen two months before. We have always been each other's best friend, and we still are, but somehow it seemed to me perfectly natural that we should come apart just as we had gone together, casually almost without any sentiment or excitement. Craig said he would write, and I knew he wouldn't and knew as well that the moment I saw him again we would be right away as good friends as ever we had been. So Craig went home the third week in September, and I stayed on in Paris with the slow-flowing Seine and the shadow of black Sambo down the hall.

As the boat train was just pulling out of the Gare St. Lazare, Craig leaned out the window and started to spout some sort of slush about what our being together had meant to him, but I said, "Stuff it, Alexander, stuff it!" and Craig laughed and shouted "O. K., Boss," as the train rolled away from me down the platform.

For about a week after Craig had gone I felt as though something inside me was going around without any clothes on, but soon it began to get itself dressed, and by October Craig had gotten to be for me just part of Springfield, though often at unexpected moments I suddenly remembered things about him—the way he had of summing up a discussion with a bad epigram and the way he had of running his fingers along a wall or a fence when we were walking.

I had a long letter from him from the boat full of unconvincing explanations which seemed entirely natural. He said that of course it had been a wonderful experience, and that he couldn't thank me enough for all the help I had been to him, but that he was convinced that, although he would always want to live a life of the spirit and the intellect, he wasn't really gifted for poetry and that probably he had just mistaken sensitivity for something more. He ended up by saying that he knew I had real talent and that I shouldn't let myself be discouraged by what he imagined was just a normal interval of lying fallow.

I didn't reread his letter, but I didn't throw it away, because I could see that he'd spent a lot of time on it, probably making two or three drafts to get it right.

Then there was the letter from Springfield saying that the town hadn't razzed him half as much as he'd expected and that most of the people were really a good deal better sort than he'd thought. Later he wrote from Chicago that his father had agreed to put him through the university so that he could get a teaching job, and then there was nothing for about five months, until I got one of those fancy engagement announcements in three envelopes. It was a girl I'd never liked much, but her father had a big drygoods business and she'd been East to school. On the corner of the card Craig had written in pencil "How'm I doin?" with three big dollar signs after it. I thought about the dollar signs and thought about some of the poems he had written, and then I didn't think anymore because I saw there was really nothing to think about.

For a while after Craig had gone I went on with my quiet life, watching the flow of the city living, slow as the flow of the river, waiting for nothing, as the Parisians seemed to be waiting for nothing, and as their river the Seine seemed not to be knowing that it was flowing or where it was going. For a while, I say, things were as they had been, except that I was doing them alone and a little sadly. And then I too began to change, though not as Craig had changed. I didn't rebel at the movement around me, or fight against it as he had done, I simply began to become a part of it, to move with it and in it, to go as it flowed, to be one with it. Still I was watching the waiting, but now the two were one thing; the watching became my waiting. I was no longer waiting for nothing because I was watching, but because my watching was in time with my waiting, I was not waiting as Americans wait, waiting for something to happen, I was waiting as Parisians wait, awaiting nothing and yet always having something, having my watching and then finally another thing—my telling.

Yes, again the top came off my typewriter and I bought hundreds of sheets of white paper, and again my writing began. But now it was different than it had been before, it was a part of the very flowing it described. It was no longer a means to something, but something itself, no longer something I was waiting to have happen, to have succeed, to win me fame and escape from Springfield; it was, as I say, no longer this to me, it was a constant part of life to me, something I did each day as I ate and sat and talked and watched and waited. It came to be not telling life for me, but part of life itself for me.

And so as fall came on and the heat of summer fell away, I came to be working every day, telling the things I saw and what I thought I knew about them, making a picture of this slow and steady movement, this gradual onward flowing, this simple waiting that I felt and lived. As the leaves fell and the night grew cold, as each day the lights came on a little earlier, as each day the air told more of winter's coming, as each day there was less struggle inside me between what remained of the life at home and what was building of my own life, I came to have, to really have and really know, what we had tried so hard to find and never found, I came to be a writer and began to be a man.

NOTES ON CONTRIBUTORS

BETSY ADAMS has published two books of poetry. A section of her novel, *the dead birth, itself,* appeared in *ND42,* and her poem sequence, "Face at the Bottom of the World," was included in *ND38.*

For information on MAX AUB, see the translator's introduction to "The Manuscript of a Crow." New Directions brought out WILL KIRKLAND's translation of Federico García Lorca's *The Cricket Sings: Poems and Songs for Children* in 1981.

A translator from the French and one of the prime exponents of Symbolist poetry in China, BIAN ZHILIN (b. 1910) produced most of his poetic *oeuvre* during the 1930s. He is now a member of the Research Institute of Foreign Languages and Literature in the Chinese Academy of Sciences. EUGENE EOYANG chairs the Department of East Asian Languages and Cultures at Indiana University. He is an editor of the journal *Chinese Literature: Essays, Articles, Reviews* and the *Yearbook of Comparative and General Literature. Sunflower Splendor: Three Thousand Years of Chinese Poetry* (Doubleday/ Anchor, 1975) contains many of his translations.

EDWIN BROCK is poetry editor of the English literary magazine *Ambit,* and his poems have appeared in such American magazines as *The New Yorker, Antaeus,* and *Partisan Review.* New Directions has published his satirical *Paroxisms* and four books of poetry.

ABELARDO CASTILLO was born in a suburb of Buenos Aires in 1935. His plays and stories have won accolades throughout Latin America, including first commendation of the eleventh Casa de las Américas competition (1961), the Medal of Honor of the Society of Argentinian Writers (1961), and the International Prize of Contemporary Latin American Dramatists (1963). GREGORY WOODRUFF has published translations of stories by Mario Benedetti, Leopoldo Lugones,

Marco Deveni, and Adolfo Bioy-Casares, and, in collaboration with Donald Yates, Bioy-Casares' novel *Diary of the War of the Pig*.

The editor and publisher of *Origen*, CID CORMAN's poetry, criticism, and translations have been published by New Directions and Black Sparrow, among others. His latest collection of poems is *AEGIS* (Station Hill Press, 1981).

FUMIKO ENCHI (b. 1905) began her literary career as a playwright and has published a modern Japanese translation of *The Tale of Genji*, but she is principally known for her fiction. "A Bond for Two Lifetimes—Gleanings" was published in Japanese in 1957. PHYLLIS BIRNBAUM's translation of the story is included in *Rabbits, Crabs, Etc.*, her anthology of stories by Japanese women, published this year by the University Press of Hawaii. Her novel, *An Eastern Tradition* (Seaview Books), came out in 1980.

New Directions brought out LAWRENCE FERLINGHETTI's *Endless Life: Selected Poems*, and a limited edition of his travel journal, *A Trip to Italy and France*, in 1981.

Born in the mid-1880s, DORA GABE is one of Bulgaria's best-loved poets. She studied literature abroad, and on her return, helped found the Bulgarian Center of International PEN. Since her first poetry collection in 1928, *Earthly Way*, she has published prose and verse for both children and adults. JASCHA KESSLER teaches English and modern literature at U.C.L.A. He has received both the Hungarian PEN Club Medal (1979) and Artisjus Award (1980). Besides translations, he is the author of stories, novels and, most recently, *Transmigrations* (Jazz Press), a book of eighteen fictive poems. A professor of English at Sophia University, ALEXANDER SHURBANOV has translated Chaucer's *The Canterbury Tales* and Milton's *Paradise Lost* into Bulgarian.

JAMES B. HALL is a novelist, poet, and fiction writer. Among his collections of stories are *The Short Hall* (Stonehenge Books, 1981) and *Us He Devours* (New Directions/San Francisco Review, 1964).

SAMUEL HAZO directs the International Poetry Forum, Pittsburgh, and is a professor of English at Duquesne University. New Directions brought out his most recent book of poems, *To Paris*, in 1980.

Information on WILLIAM HEINESEN can be found in the translator's introduction to the poems in this volume and preceding Heinesen's stories in *ND38* and *ND40*. HEDIN BRØNNER's books and articles on Scandinavian literature have appeared in the United States and Norway. His translation of *The Wingéd Darkness and Other Stories*, by William Heinesen, will appear shortly.

LÊDO IVO's collected poems were published in 1976 in his native Brazil, where he is celebrated as a translator, journalist, and poetic spokesman of the "Generation of 1945." His first book to appear in this country was the novel *Snakes' Nest* (New Directions, 1981), translated by Kern Krapohl. JON TOLMAN, who contributed an introduction to *Snakes' Nest*, teaches at the University of New Mexico. KERRY SHAWN KEYES's translation of João Cabral de Melo Neto's "A Knife All Blade" appeared in *ND44*.

HAROLD JAFFE's fiction, poetry, and criticism has appeared in *Chicago Review, Fiction, Fiction International, Minnesota Review, Poetry Northwest, The Nation,* and *The New York Times*. He is codirector of the Fiction Collective.

TERRY KISTLER is president of Poets & Writers, Inc. His poems have appeared in *Harper's Magazine, Nimrod,* and two anthologies—*The 1981 Anthology of American Verse and Modern Poetry* and *Timeless Voices*.

Exiled from his native East Germany soon after the publication of his second novel in 1976, REINER KUNZE is the author of five volumes of poetry which have won numerous honors, including the Bavarian Academy of Arts literature award (1973) and the Georg Büchner Prize (1977) as well as awards from Czechoslovakia, Sweden, and Austria. LORI FISHER's translations of Kunze's poetry have been published by Swamp Press, *Buckle Magazine,* and *Footprints*. She makes her home in Iowa City.

JAMES LAUGHLIN is president and publisher of New Directions.

A lifelong friend of the late Thomas Merton, ROBERT LAX has lived on the Greek island of Kalymnos for many years. Excerpts from his *Journals* have appeared in *ND31* and elsewhere. *The Circus of the Sun, Oedipus, Thought,* and *New Poems,* his books of verse, were all brought out by Journeyman Press. Professor ROBERT BUTMAN makes his home in Haverford, Pennsylvania.

DAVID ZANE MAIROWITZ was born in New York, spent the last fifteen years in London, and recently moved to the south of France. His fiction has appeared in *Penguin Modern Stories 11, Partisan Review, Tri-Quarterly, Chicago Review, Fiction,* and *In the Slipstream* (Chicago Review Press), and his plays have been produced in London and Los Angeles. Among his nonfiction works is *The Radical Soap Opera,* on the American Left (Avon, 1977).

A founder of the Italian *avant-garde* "Gruppo '63," GIORGIO MANGANELLI published his first book, *Hilarotragedia,* in 1964. This was followed by nine works of fiction and nonfiction, including *Centuria: One Hundred Little Sagas,* winner of the prestigious Italian Viareggio prize in 1979, parts of which are included in this volume. Manganelli is also a leading critic and journalist and teaches American literature at the University of Rome. KATHERINE JASON's poems and translations have appeared in *The New Yorker, Translation, Midstream,* and elsewhere. After receiving an M.F.A. from the Columbia University Writing Program in 1978, she traveled to Italy on a Fulbright-Hays grant.

Since his first collection, *Color of Darkness* (New Directions, 1957), JAMES PURDY has been a strong presence on the literary scene. Viking/Penguin, which published his most recent novel, *Mourners Below* (1980), will be bringing out his newest book, *On Glory's Course,* in 1983.

BORISLAV RADOVIĆ was born in 1935 in Belgrade, Yugoslavia, and still lives in that city. He has five books of poetry to his credit. ALEKSANDAR NEJGEBAUER lives in Novi Sad. His two books of verse are *Haikus* (1975) and *Time Measures* (1978).